Richard Baron

Well begun is half done

The young painter and Fiddlehanns

Richard Baron

Well begun is half done
The young painter and Fiddlehanns

ISBN/EAN: 9783337197537

Printed in Europe, USA, Canada, Australia, Japan

Cover: Foto ©Andreas Hilbeck / pixelio.de

More available books at **www.hansebooks.com**

WELL BEGUN IS HALF DONE,

OR

THE YOUNG PAINTER;

AND

FIDDLEHANNS.

TALES TRANSLATED FROM THE GERMAN OF

RICHARD BARON AND DR. C. DEUTSCH.

BY

Trauermantel.

NEW YORK:

P. O'SHEA, PUBLISHER,

97 BARCLAY STREET.

DEDICATION.

DEAR AGNES : —

I scarcely venture, with your maturing years and already ripened intellect, to dedicate to you a book for children. And yet I feel quite sure you will find pleasure in the simple but lofty lessons taught in the accompanying beautiful tales, as well as appreciate the affection which leads me to wish to see your name at their head.

Sincerely yours,

THE TRANSLATOR.

CONTENTS.

WELL BEGUN IS HALF DONE,

OR

THE YOUNG PAINTER.

CHAPTER I.

THE village school of Reichenthal was not a whit less bustling and noisy than most country schools of its class, and at the particular time of the commencement of our story the humble walls re-echoed with the usual din ; the humming of many youthful voices, studying, reciting, or indulging in the delights of a stolen and whispered interchange of views and opinions.

The master was walking up and down before his scholars, and eloquently expounding the mysteries of the noble art of calculation. His discourse was frequently interrupted by questions, which were sometimes addressed to single individuals, and sometimes were expected to be answered by a band of united voices, all the boys and girls joining in full chorus.

Suddenly, the zealous master arrested his course, and fastened a sharp glance upon one of the boys in the front row. The child hastily strove to conceal a paper beneath the table.

"What can that troublesome boy have been scribbling at again?" cried the master. "Out with it!"

The boy blushed deeply, cast an imploring glance upon the master's face, and stammered a few unintelligible words, while his neighbors on either hand secretly tittered among themselves.

"Out with it, I tell you! Some stupid thing, I'll warrant. Come, make haste!"

The little culprit trembled as he slowly drew forth a sheet of paper from beneath the table. The master seized it, placed his spectacles upon his great nose, and with an ominous shake of the head regarded the image which met his view.

"What is this?" he finally cried. "I actually believe the boy has been intending to caricature me! As true as I live! And what

a nose he has given me. Ah! you little rascal,
is this the way you make fun of your master?"

"Pardon! pardon!" begged the boy, imploringly lifting his beautiful eyes, now suffused
with tears.

"Yes, pardon! That is what you always
say. How many thousand times have I told
you to quit this eternal sketching and caricatur-
ing! But every scrap of paper that falls into
the boy's clutches is covered in a trice with
dogs, horses, houses, even men's heads, — and
I must confess they look so natural that one
might almost fancy them real!"

"Ah! dear master," cried the boy, "indeed
I cannot help it."

"Cannot help it! Come here, and I will
show you that you both can and must help it!
Look! — you have drawn me with a fine rod
in my hand! You shall find that I do not
carry it for nothing. Come here, sir!"

Then followed a short castigation, to which
the little sketcher patiently and humbly submitted. He then returned to his place, and
when the interrupted lesson was again resumed,
his attention and the correctness of his answers

1*

showed that he could not only make pictures, but that he was also well advanced in the more practical branches of education.

The bell finally rang, and school was out. The children rushed joyously into the open play-ground.   Gustavus, — for such was the boy's name, — in obedience to the master's command, remained behind.

"Gustavus," said the latter, "I punished you to-day because you chose me, your master, as a subject for ridicule.   In the Word of God stands the law : 'Thou shalt honor thy father and thy mother,' and this law includes thy superiors !   Do you comprehend that ? "

" Yes, I understand it, and I beseech you to forgive me ! " said the boy, with unaffected contrition.

" Well then, — you are forgiven.   But, for Heaven's sake, tell me what all this everlasting drawing and painting means ?   In other respects you are a very sensible boy.   You read like a mill-clapper, you reckon like a clerk, you learn your hymns and verses better than any of the others, and you write almost as well as your master.   And yet you will not quit covering your books and every wall and barn door with your endless scribbling. Hey, now! How is all this to end?"

"I do not know," replied Gustavus. "But you see, dear master, my head is always filled with so many strange pictures. Day and night, waking and sleeping, they dance before my eyes, and give me no rest. Then something forces me to seize on the first pen or pencil, bit of chalk or charcoal, I can find, and note down with my fingers all that is passing through my brain. And then I feel so happy! Oh! *so* happy!"

The master shook his head.

"This is a wonderful gift of God, which may readily become very dangerous to you. Your mother tells me that you are very idle at home, and that you give her a great deal of trouble."

The boy's eyes filled with tears. "Ah!" cried he, "that is very true; both father and mother are often dissatisfied with me. I hate chopping and digging, spinning and looking after the cows. I want to go out into the wide, wide world. I want—I know not exactly what!"

"Come, come," said the master, kindly,
"compose yourself! The world is indeed
very wide, and you are still a very young and
a totally inexperienced lad. The world is like
a great shark with a monstrous pair of jaws, —
it might easily swallow you down, skin and
hair and all! The best thing for you will be
to stay at home and perform all your duties.
And now go, and remember this command-
ment: 'Children, obey your parents for the
sake of the Lord!'"

Gustavus went, and with the usual elasticity
of youth, soon recovered from the painful impressions produced by the conversation held
with his master. He rapidly hastened toward
his father's cottage, which, surrounded by its
pretty garden, lay on the outskirts of the village. Behind it rose a lofty eminence, and the
little side windows looked out upon a noble
forest of oaks and beeches.

"Mother!" cried the boy to a woman clad
in the ordinary dress of the peasants in that
part of the country, — "mother, I will dig and
delve to-day with all my might; only let me
have the spade and the rake that I may finish
something worth speaking of before noon."

Ere the mother, according to her usual custom, had time to warn him against idleness and day-dreaming, he was already in the garden, and the dexterity with which he handled the implements proved that he not only possessed a nobly gifted intellect, but that God had also endowed him with a strong and healthy body.

We will leave him at his work, and inquire a little more closely into his actual condition and circumstances; for our young readers will already have divined that he is to be the hero of our tale.

Braun, Gustavus's foster-father, — for such was the real connection between the boy and the peasant, — was an under forester in the royal service. This post had been conferred upon him as a reward for his good conduct during the recent war. The salary, however, was very small, and barely sufficed to keep his family above the pressure of actual want. In addition to Gustavus, he had five children of his own, and the little household could scarcely have continued to exist, had not Braun's exertions been aided by the industry and careful management of his wife.

Gustavus was the father's darling, — but by
no means the mother's.   An impenetrable mystery shrouded his origin.   All that was known
was, that when Braun had returned from the
wars, he had brought the child with him.   But
where or how he had come into his possession
had either never been related, or had been forgotten.   In short, Gustavus was regarded as
Braun's adopted son, and no further consideration was bestowed upon the subject   Braun
had not married until after his return, and the
boy had failed in winning his adopted mother's
love.   The peasant woman was by no means
ill disposed, but the affection she bore her own
offspring so entirely filled her heart, that she
had none to spare for the little stranger.

When she found her family increasing very
rapidly, and began to fear lest there should be
some difficulty in providing for them all, Gustavus only appeared to her in the light of an
unwelcome intruder who had no claim upon
her care or attention.   In addition to this, the
child's peculiarities of mind and temperament,
as they had early developed themselves, were
in direct opposition to all the ideas, and even

the very nature, of the active and industrious woman. When little more than an infant, Gustavus had displayed traits of character un-usual in a peasant boy; he preferred to wander alone through the neighboring wood, and for hours together would watch the gay sports of the birds, the squirrels, the deer, or other liv-ing creatures abounding in the forest, or, lying at the foot of some tall tree, he would seem never to weary of gazing upon the dancing leaves, the blue sky, or the floating clouds.

When he grew older, he was seized with an unconquerable desire of imitating with his pencil everything he saw; and, rough as the sketches were, they excited universal astonish-ment from their spirit and exactitude. The cottage and outbuildings bore numberless traces of the boy's peculiar mania. On the barn door, a lusty cavalier was seen galloping away on a spirited steed, a troop of cavalry which had shortly before passed through the village having afforded the model. As a com-panion to this, was a sketch of a traveller mounted on an ass, whose picturesque appear-ance and appointments for mountain travel

had attracted the boy's fancy. The white-
washed cottage walls were covered with scenes
from the Old Testament, evidently copied from
the pictures in the village church. The peak
of the roof was adorned with a variety of comi-
cal figures, modelled in clay, and representing
men or animals. Neither the stranger nor the
villager could pass by the little dwelling without glancing upward, and bestowing a smile or
a look of wonder upon this singular assemblage
of images; and endless were the questions
asked concerning the artist who had conceived
and executed so many curious and beautiful
designs.

We may readily imagine that these favorite
pursuits cost Gustavus many precious hours,
and also that they were a source of unceasing
contention with his foster-mother, who would
have much preferred seeing him, in winter, at
the spinning-wheel; and in summer, caring for
the cows and goats, or laboring in the garden.
She thought the little stranger in duty bound to
earn the bread which he consumed, and whenever Gustavus stole away from his work to his
beloved pictures, the transgression was speed-

ily followed by many and loud reproaches, not infrequently accompanied by corporal punishment. The father, too, when in the evening he returned from the forest, was often assailed with a volley of complaints, and much domestic eloquence was he forced to expend in pacifying the good dame, and in moderating her indignation at "that idle, good-for-nothing, scribbling lad," as she called Gustavus, whose designs were in her eyes nothing more than the marring of unsullied walls, and the soiling of clean places with useless dirt.

Thus, among many joys and many sorrows, had Gustavus grown into an active, spirited, and healthy boy. It was a real pleasure to look upon his fine, open countenance, from which shone two clear, dark eyes, and round which waved a profusion of graceful brown curls. All his motions, his walk, and his language, were marked by a certain grace and elegance which advantageously distinguished him from the other village boys of his own age. And if drawing and painting were his favorite occupations, yet, aided by his excellent memory and quick understanding, he had readily ac-

quired all that was to be learned in the village
school.

He had also eagerly devoured several works
on history owned by his father, and sundry
treatises on natural history lent him by the
village pastor, with whom he was a great
favorite. He was thus well advanced for his
years and circumstances, and the travellers
whom he sometimes guided over the neighboring mountain were always surprised at the
quickness of his perceptions, the soundness of
his judgment, and his tasteful and accurate use
of language.

He also possessed a good heart and a kind
and loving disposition. Even his foster-mother's want of affection, and rough treatment,
had failed in exciting the faintest emotion of
bitterness in his soul; indeed, his gentleness
and submission not infrequently disarmed the
good dame's anger, when she fancied herself
especially aggrieved through his love of reverie, or the ill-timed pursuit of his favorite art.

He treated his little brothers and sisters
most affectionately; he protected them, played
with them, and rejoiced their innocent hearts

with all manner of little figures daintily fashioned from wood or bark. His deepest feelings, however, were all devoted to his foster-father, who, although a plain and unlearned man, had heart and mind enough to recognize the boy's superior gifts, and to love him as if he had been his own son.

We will now return to our hero, in whose behalf we hope this short account will have excited the sympathy of our readers. The sun shone down bright and warm from the heavens as the boy pursued his laborious task of digging trenches, which he then carefully filled with tender young plants. But his heart was not in his work. His imagination was revelling in some far distant scenes, and was filled with an endless succession of lovely pictures.

Gustavus had a few days before guided several travellers across the mountain, and the loveliness of the scenery through which he had passed was ever before him. Also, the travellers had been so lively, and had treated the bright, intelligent boy so kindly, that wherever he turned he saw their benevolent faces with his inward eye. "O, if I could only paint

you now, you dear, good people!" thought
Gustavus. "Well, so I could, for you stand
before me as if you were actually about to
speak. But I cannot satisfy myself with chalk
and coal! Ah! if I only had a piece of clean
white paper, with a pencil, a brush, and some
colors! — Well, I will try just once! — But
no," continued he, again seizing upon the
spade which he had left standing in the trench;
" no, I promised my mother to work steadily
on until noon. She shall not always be forced
to scold me as an idle, lazy boy!"

He continued to dig, but the thought of
drawing his dear travelling companions was too
enticing, — the temptation proved too strong.

"I can easily spare a couple of minutes, I
can then work twice as fast," thought he, as he
slipped away towards the door of an enclosure
which still offered him a smooth, unsullied sur-
face. He found a piece of charcoal in his
pocket, and hastily began his work. He had
already sketched a huge rock, at whose foot
the company were to be placed; the beautiful
lady and the venerable old man with the long
beard were already drawn . . . . .

When suddenly the shrill voice of his foster-mother fell upon his ear, scolding in no gentle tones. "Just look!" she cried, "just look at that good-for-nothing boy. I fancy him working in the garden like a reasonable Christian, and there he is lounging at the barn doors, and scratching them all over with his frightful puppets!"

We will spare our young readers the flood of reproaches which overwhelmed the poor lad. Gustavus slipped quietly away, really ashamed at his own forgetfulness, and ready to do anything to show his sorrow and avert the storm.

During the remainder of this day, and the next following, no more industrious, willing, and obliging boy than Gustavus showed himself to be could be found in any household or in any school-room.

2*

CHAPTER II.

TIME passed, and Gustavus was now about fourteen years old, circumstances rendering it impossible to determine exactly the date of his birth. On the morning of that joyful day which we commemorate in honor of our Lord's ascension, the boy had received the Sacrament of confirmation.

During the afternoon of the same day the father threw his gun over his shoulder, called the boy, and bade him accompany him to the wood, as he had much to say to him. They went, and were soon walking together beneath the spreading branches of the lofty birches, oaks, and beeches, which, although devoid of foliage, yet by the swelling of their buds already announced the joyful approach of spring. Above them was the clear blue heaven, whence shone the sun so bright and warm that all nature seemed to feel the call to a renewal of life and activity ; the first spring birds twittered, the numerous tribes of insects and harmless reptiles began to creep out of their secret recesses, and the earliest flowers peeped up with their tender, bright little eyes through the dry moss and dead leaves. It was one of those lovely days when the power of God seems to breathe anew athwart creation, endowing all his works with new beauty and vigor. At such times, too, the hearts of men are filled with strange divinings, and lifted far above the sordid cares of earth on the wings of blissful emotion.

They finally came to a small clearing on the summit of a hill, whence their eyes could wander over the wide-spread forest lying at their feet, with its singing brooks, lovely valleys, and scattered villages.

" Let us sit here ! " said the father. " 'T is a holy day, and the wild creatures of the wood

shall also rest; I only hope the poachers and
wood-thieves will leave me a little repose. I
have many important things to talk to thee
about, Gustavus."

They sat down upon the trunk of a fallen
tree. Gustavus gazed silently and expectantly
into his father's honest face. The good man
began as follows:—"This has been a happy day
for me. My heart overflowed with joy when I
saw thee stand before the altar, and heard thee
saw thee stand before the altar, and there
renew thy vow to remain a faithful and upright
servant of thy Saviour, of that Holy One whom
we men are all bound through life and death
to follow. All my hopes with regard to thee
have been fulfilled. And yet my heart is full
of anxiety on thy account."

"On my account? How, father, have I
given thee cause for sorrow?"

"No, thou hast given me no cause! But thy
future fate occasions me much anxiety. Gustavus, what is to become of thee?"

The boy made no reply; his head sank, and
his eyes were thoughtfully fixed upon the
ground.

"Thou seest, my boy, thy life henceforth

must be very different from what it has hitherto been. Thou art no longer a child. Thou
hast left thy school days behind thee, and it
will not be well for thee longer to remain beneath my roof."

"Thou art right, father!" cried Gustavus.
"I must go! Ah! I have long enough been
a burden to you all!"

"Say not so! Thou hast never been a burden to me. I have always considered thee as
a gift from heaven, and God is my witness that
I have never for one single moment repented
having taken thee to my heart when I bore
thee in my arms from the bloody battle-field,
and most probably, by so doing, saved thy
life."

"I know it! I know it!" cried Gustavus,
with great tears standing in his eyes. "Thou
hast always been my kind and faithful father,
and I thank thee for all — all! But thou art
poor, father! Thou hast more than enough
to do to provide for those who have a nearer
claim upon thee than I. I then can, and will,
no longer be a burden to thee."

"Speak no more of that. As long as I have

a morsel of bread, Gustavus, there will always
be a share for thee. But we must view this
matter from a different point of view. Thou
must have some settled occupation, some opportunity for advancement."

"And what dost thou think I had better
be?" asked the boy, gazing intently upon his
father's face.

"I have thought much upon the subject.
We must here do, not so much what we would
desire, as what we can and must. I long
nourished the hope that we would one day
discover thy parents. At first, I made every
possible effort — all in vain — and then I
thought some accident might perhaps throw
us upon their traces. I now see that such
hopes are vain and idle. I believe that the
rank and circumstances amid which thou wert
born are no longer possibilities for thee; thou
must then cheerfully renounce all thought of
them, and take life as God has willed it for
thee. Thou art the son of Braun, the poor
forester of Reichenthal, and, as thy father, I
can only say to thee, thou must learn a
trade!"

"Learn a trade!" repeated Gustavus in a low tone, at the same time emitting a deep sigh.

"I feared, indeed, that my proposition would not please thee. But I see no other path open. Thou knowest I can afford thee but very little assistance. Thou must open a way for thyself which will one day lead thee to an independent hearthstone of thine own. Believe me, every trade may lead to a gold mine! Industry, skill, and uprightness must insure success. But perhaps thou thinkest thyself too good for a trade! Such an idea would really pain me deeply.

"I know many a mechanic who, in God's eyes, is worth much more than many an idler clothed in silk, and taking his ease in a gilded chariot. The main point is, that thou shouldst be a good, honest, and religious man. I think a shoemaker, a weaver, or a carpenter can serve God, enjoy life, and benefit his fellow-men as well as his more aspiring brother mortals. What sayest thou to that?"

"O, thou art right, quite right! But, dear father, do not think me silly or absurd.. I fear it will be impossible for me ever to become a mechanic."

The father sadly shook his head. " I feared this," said he, as if speaking to himself. " The lad has a proud heart; he must have been born with it. I may perhaps have erred in suffering him too far to follow the bent of his own inclinations. My consideration for him as the possible offspring of noble parents is now bringing its own punishment. — Well, speak then, and tell me what thy plans are," added he, after a short pause.

" Thou seest, father, if one desires to learn and skilfully practise the simplest trade, one must possess both love and capacity for one's business : I feel within me neither inclination nor capacity. By capacity I do not mean the power which lies in the hands or the feet : of that I possess an abundance ; but I now speak of that inner power which can alone guide a man in the production of anything worthy or excellent. I should most certainly be the most awkward, useless, and unhappy mechanic living."

" Gustavus ! Gustavus ! " cried Braun, mournfully shaking his head. "Dost thou then intend to do nothing, to be of no use in the world?"

"O no, father! I feel something within me, — something I can neither name nor describe, but which tells me that my life will not have been in vain, and that no shame will ever tarnish my name. It drives me out into the world. I must go hence. O surely, I will discover and win all that now renders me both happy and unhappy, and waking or sleeping leaves me no repose."

"But unless thou intendest to be a mere dreamer, a forlorn wanderer upon the face of the earth, thou must determine upon something definite."

"I will be a painter!"

The father lifted his hands in amazement. "A painter!" cried he, — "a painter! And this is my reward! Have I not always rejoiced in the lad's drawing and painting, and now must that very talent bring me only anxiety and sorrow?"

"Yes, father, I will be a painter! Do not think this an idea of to-day or yesterday. No, it has filled my mind for years. I have never

seen a picture without feeling a desire either to
have painted it, or to be able to copy it. Whenever my eyes fell upon any lovely scene or image, my fingers burned to transfer it to paper or
canvas. Dost thou think a merciful God would
have gifted me with this intense longing, had
it not been intended to serve some good purpose? Is it not our duty to employ to the
best advantage the talent with which we have
been intrusted?"

"Ah, Gustavus, into what a sea of troubles
thy foolish passion for painting plunges me!
Even allowing thee to have the natural gifts
requisite to success, where art thou to find the
means of pursuing thy studies, and where
wilt thou find a master? How canst thou
overcome the thousand obstacles which lie in
thy path? Thou seemest to me like one who
sees afar off a glittering palace which he has
set his heart upon reaching, forgetful of the
broad, deep stream rolling at his feet, with
neither bridge nor boat to bear him across the
turbid waters. And even shouldst thou succeed in reaching the goal, it might turn out to
be a mere air castle.".

"No, father!" cried Gustavus. "As I stood this morning before the altar, penetrated with a devout and prayerful joy, and as I earnestly implored of God the fulfilment of my heart's desire, my soul was so filled with a holy peace and a cheerful confidence, that I now feel quite sure of attaining my end. 'Seek and you shall find, ask and you shall receive!' Hast thou not often reminded me of that saying of our Lord's?"

"But, Gustavus, I must again repeat that I see no possibility of thy finding the necessary means. How wilt thou even begin?"

"I will tell thee all as I have thought it out. Grant me one year, dear father! I will go to Breslau, and will seek a master. I will not cease my search until I have succeeded. O, father! It cannot be that every door and every heart will be closed against me! When I have found one willing to take pity on a poor boy, I will study, labor, and paint, so that the very angels in heaven will rejoice over my success. But if I am disappointed, if I find no master, or if I see that I can do nothing worthy of thy son, I will return at the end of the year,

and will consent to become whatever thou
mayest desire."

The father thoughtfully shook his head.
" No, no," cried he, after a pause," that will
never do.   It would be a sin in me to let thee
thus depart.   Only think !   Thou art so young
to be thrown into the turmoil of this bewildering world !   If thou shouldst meet with any
mishap, or if, through thy very innocence and
want of experience, thou shouldst be led into
sin, or tempted into evil ways ! My heart is
ready to break at the very thought ! "

" Is that thy fear ?   O, dearest father, banish
it far from thee.   Dost thou know me no better ?   Hast thou not thyself taught me to hate
evil from the bottom of my heart, and to keep
God ever before my eyes and in my soul ?
Hear me, father !   By that God who has arched
the blue of his glorious heavens above our
heads, by that Saviour to whom I have this
day vowed eternal fidelity, I promise thee to
keep my heart and my hand from all unright-
eousness.   Thy Gustavus will always so conduct himself that thou wilt never have reason
to be ashamed of him ! "

The boy had risen to his feet. Such joyful assurance, such depth and truth of holy resolution shone in his countenance, that the father could no longer resist.

"A man's will is his most sacred possession!" said he. "I know not what, in spite of my better reason, impels me to yield to thy foolish desire. Thou mayest then depart. It is not impossible that the voice of thy heart may be the voice of God calling thee for thine own good."

"Thou consentest! Thou consentest! Oh! now all will be well!" joyfully cried Gustavus. He threw himself into his father's arms, and fairly overwhelmed him with kisses and caresses. Braun finally withdrew himself from the boy's passionate demonstrations of gratitude.

"Come, come, my son!" said he, "we must give this matter further consideration. We must also ask counsel of thy mother. And now, sit down and listen to me. If thou art about to leave us, it is doubly necessary that I should relate to thee precisely how, in the wonderful ways of Providence, thou chancedst

3 *

to become my son. Hitherto, all that thou hast known is, that I found thee, an infant, upon the battle-field of Leipsic."

This recall to the melancholy and mysterious circumstances overshadowing his early life at once banished every trace of the joyous animation beaming from the boy's countenance. A new and solemn interest took its place as he silently seated himself by his father's side. Braun thus began his narration : —

" The last battle of Leipsic was a warmly contested day. The armies waved to and fro, like two seas driven one against the other by opposing winds. The French fought with the energy of despair, and every foot of ground we won was covered with the corpses of our fallen enemies. But we strove with God, for our king and country, and our foes were finally forced to give way. It was still early in the afternoon when the French began to fall back upon the Rhine. Those regiments which had lost the fewest men were ordered to continue the pursuit. We pressed vigorously onward, continually harassing the flying enemy, until their ranks fell into the wildest disorder.

"Great God! what horrible sights met our
eyes! The roads, far and near, to the right
and the left, were strewn with dead and dying
men, with dead horses, and abandoned or disabled cannons and baggage-wagons. It was
a scene of such horrible and heart-rending confusion, that to this day my flesh creeps whenever
I think of it. Ah, Gustavus, man is fearful
when he meets his brother man upon a battle-
field, where a human life weighs no more than
a feather in the scale! The events of that one
day at Leipsic cost half a world millions of
tears. But little did we think of that; our
every nerve was strained to do all possible
injury to our enemies, and not to allow them a
moment's repose.

"It was toward evening when we reached a
place where the struggle had been long and
desperate, but where the French had at length
been overcome. The desolation was fearful.
Our way led over heaps of slain, and fragments
of every kind of military appurtenance. A
disabled coach lying in the road especially attracted our attention. My comrades hoped to
find a valuable booty, and quickly surrounded

and sacked the carriage; I stood at a little distance. Suddenly I heard a laugh, and a loud
cry of 'a child! a child!' I sprang forward.
In fact, an infant lay sleeping in a tiny bed on
the back seat of the carriage. That was indeed a
strange sight! Only think; amid those bloody
and murderous scenes, surrounded by rude
and bearded warriors, lay the child, beautiful
as an angel, and peacefully sleeping as if repos-
ing in the arms of God! Truly, it was neither
the time nor the place to busy one's self with
children, but that sight touched every fibre in
my heart. Brothers! cried I, that is my share
of the booty! I took the child in my arms.
It awoke, and opening its two clear, dark eyes,
turned them full upon my face. God, thought
I, has surely watched over the life of this little
one; it would be a real child murder were I to
leave it this cold, autumnal night amid the
horrors of the battle-field. We marched on.
I fastened the infant as well as I could upon
my left shoulder, and either the child's guar-
dian angel, or the influence of its own angelic
loveliness and innocence, must have softened
the wild hearts of my comrades, for they made

to attempt to impede my progress, and refrained from the utterance of a single rude
jest."

Gustavus, who had thus far listened in
silence, could no longer control his emotion,
and burst into tears.

"I do not wonder that thou weepest, my
son," said Braun. "That child was no other
than thyself. God only knows how thou
chancedst to be in so fearful a place. I have
always supposed that where so young a child
was found, the mother, or at least the nurse,
could not be far distant. But we saw no
traces of any feminine presence. That is but
one of the many mysteries buried beneath the
bloody soil of that fatal battle-ground, and not
until the last trump shall sound, can we hope
for their revelation. — As night came on, we
reached a large village, where we rested during
a couple of hours, for we were dreadfully exhausted. My first care was to seek some safe
place of refuge for thee, as it was impossible
for me to carry thee any farther. But this
was no easy matter. Nearly all the inhabitants of the place had fled; in vain did we

knock at the doors, and when we forced them open we found only silence and desolation within. I finally succeeded in luring from his hiding-place a young peasant, whose dwelling lay upon the outskirts of the town.

"'Hey, friend!' cried I to him, 'the battle is won, and the enemy driven away, God willing, never to return. Thank God for your deliverance; and that you may show your gratitude by deeds as well as by words, I will intrust you with the care of a child I found upon the battle-field.'

"The peasant stood a moment irresolute. 'Come, come, there is no time for delay!' cried I, in a rough voice. 'I cannot take the child with me, and I will most certainly not leave it upon the cold ground to perish. Are you married?' 'Yes.' 'So much the better! Have you any children?' 'One.' 'Then you can easily take charge of a second!' At that moment a peasant woman, who had probably heard the whole conversation, crept forth from her place of concealment.

"'There, my good woman,' said I, 'take the child, and be a mother to it.'

"The woman took thee in her arms, and when she saw how forlorn and forsaken thou wert, a feeling of humanity arose in her breast, for she said : 'Poor little creature! Well, yes then, I will, will be a mother to it!' 'God in heaven reward you!' cried I, as happy as a king. 'I must now go. When the war is ended, should I still be among the living, I will certainly return and see what has become of the little fellow.'

"Well, thou wert then at least in safety, and I felt as if a heavy weight had been lifted from my heart. At the end of the two hours we again moved on. The rest of the tale thou already knowest. We drove the French over the Rhine, invaded their country, and, after many a hard fight, entered their very capital, — Paris. Peace was then declared, and we returned to our native land. Thou mayest be sure thou hadst not been forgotten. My way home led through Saxony, and of course I did not shun taking a little longer route, that I might again see thee.

"When I entered the cot where I had left thee, I saw a little boy playing in the sand.

He had an amiable countenance, a skin like
lilies and roses, and a profusion of fair, curling
locks. He was, however, very dirty, and evidently neglected. The peasant woman at that
moment made her appearance.

"'Well!' cried I, as I gave her a friendly
greeting, 'is that the boy I left with you last
year?' 'Yes, sir, that is he.' I took thee up
in my arms, and pressed a hearty kiss upon
thy lips. I was glad to see thee so strong and
healthy. But what was I to do now? Should
I take thee with me, or leave thee with those
who had thus far taken care of thee? Before
deciding, I determined to discover how thou
wert treated in the house, and especially
whether the people loved thee. For this purpose, I remained with them during the whole
day. But the household did not please me.
They were uncommonly rough people, and I
could see they cared but little for thee. They
did not even attempt to hide that they would be
very glad to be relieved of further trouble on
thy account.

" My resolution was soon taken. I then had
plenty of money. We were returning as vic-

tors, and in a foreign land, without extortion or dishonesty, had had many opportunities of increasing our little stores. I took thee with me, and engaging our passage in the post-coach from the neighboring village, soon reached my home. Until I married, my mother took charge of thee, and all the rest thou knowest."

When Braun had finished his narration, Gustavus threw himself sobbing upon his bosom.

"Ah, father!" cried he, "how good thou hast been to me! What was I to thee, that thou shouldst snatch me from destruction, and bestow so much love upon me? My daily prayer will ever be, that I may repay thee for all thou hast done for me."

"I did not do it for reward, my son. My only wish is that thou mayest be an honest and upright man. Then indeed will my joy be full at the thought of having saved thee. But I have yet one thing more to say. As I was that evening bearing thee from the field of battle, I observed a small gold chain hanging about thy neck. I drew it forth, and found attached to it a tiny gold locket. Here it is. Press this spring, and thou wilt see something that will surprise thee."

Gustavus took the locket and pressed the spring. It flew open, and his eye fell upon the portrait of a young and very lovely woman.

"It is by no means impossible," said Braun, "that that may be a portrait of thy mother."

"My mother! O my mother!" sobbed the boy, as he fervently pressed the picture to his lips.

"It is thine only inheritance from thy parents. Take it with thee. I do not dare to hope that it may aid thee in finding thy relatives, for I fancy they are more probably French than German. But the locket and chain are of considerable value, and shouldst thou at any time fall into great need, thou mightest perhaps purchase thy life by disposing of them."

Gustavus made no reply. He was sunk in profound meditation and reverie. An entirely new world seemed to have arisen in his innermost being. His eyes were fastened upon the portrait, intently studying the expression of that mild and beautiful countenance, which, with some strange power, seemed to be interpenetrating his very soul.

"My mother!" whispered he from time to time, as great tears rolled slowly over his flushed cheeks.

When his father finally called him, he rose and silently followed the good man on his homeward way.

CHAPTER III.

BRAUN was tormented during the whole of
the succeeding night with the thought that his
adopted son was about to leave him, and venture alone amid the tortuous paths of an unknown world. He almost repented having
yielded his consent, and his imagination painted
in the darkest colors the manifold dangers to
which the boy's innocence and inexperience
would be exposed. Early the next morning
he went to the pastor of the place, a pious and
experienced man, and laid before him the
whole of his doubts and difficulties. The clergyman reassured him, saying : —

" Your Gustavus is a very extraordinary
boy, and we may hence anticipate for him no

common destiny. What would prove the ruin
of a boy endowed with meaner capacities and a
weaker character may perhaps be for him the
means of superior elevation and finer culture.
He was born with a strong natural tendency
toward goodness and virtue; he has been carefully instructed in the law of God; and hence
I think we have little or nothing to apprehend
from his intercourse with the world. He will
be the less easily tempted, because evil of every
kind is repulsive to his very nature. In addition to this, he is really gifted with an extraordinary talent for painting. I never met with
a boy in whom a noble instinct had so decidedly
pointed the way to his future profession. All
his ideas, and everything he touches, involuntarily mould themselves into plastic or picto-
rial forms. Your son, in fact, could not well
be anything but a painter. In our village he
will have no opportunity of acquiring the requisite knowledge: he *must* go to the city, and
the sooner the better, for art is long, and life
is short. We will then permit him to depart.
I do not doubt his success, and that he will in
the end become a very remarkable man. Re-

member that the rarest and most precious
jewels always require the sharpest instruments,
and the most assiduous labor, to give them the
polish of which they are susceptible. The
greatest and noblest men are almost invariably
those who have been severely tried in the
school of adversity. Let us trust in God, that
he will not permit our Gustavus to be tempted
beyond his strength."

Braun departed with a lightened heart. Gustavus had meanwhile retreated to the little
corner in his father's house where he kept
his scanty stock of treasures, consisting of a
pencil, a few paints, some bits of white paper,
and a portfolio, which he had himself made
and carefully ornamented. This pretty effort
of the boy's invention contained his little store
of fixtures, a portion of which he had purchased with his scanty savings from itinerant
picture-dealers, while the remainder had from
time to time been given him by various persons
who had been struck with his aptitude and
fondness for the noble arts of coloring and
design. Here, also, were some of his own attempts, neatly executed on white paper, and

colored with all the taste possible, considering the meagre contents of his paint-box.

Hitherto his portfolio had been his most dearly prized earthly possession, but he now regarded the locket containing the lovely portrait as a treasure far more precious than any he had previously called his own. That he might never be parted from it, he fastened the chain round his neck, and placed the locket on his breast, beneath his clothes.

But he was also determined not to part with his portfolio, and hence was very busy in arranging its contents, and laying aside all that seemed to him unworthy of preservation. Many pictures were promptly decided upon, while others caused him much thought and many regrets. All were in fact beloved confidants, reminding him of some happy hour, when he had felt inspired to create some durable memorial of his fleeting impressions.

O ye rich! Had ye seen the boy thus occupied, lowly stooping over his treasures scattered upon the bare floor, with his happy face, and his heart fairly bubbling over with joyous hopes, — the poor boy, who could call nothing

his own, save a vigorous frame and a richly
gifted soul, — had ye seen how he associated
a happy and glorious future with these few
childish efforts, ye would surely have opened
your coffers, and thence have procured for him
an entrance to the noble kingdom of Art, and
the means of attaining the proud height to
which nature had destined him!

Who could be happier than Gustavus, when
on his father's return he learned that the pastor had not only approved of his design, but
had succeeded in allaying all the good forester's doubts and fears. The cottagers were
soon busily engaged in making the necessary
preparations for the boy's journey. To the
honor of the mother, we must say, that she had
great difficulty in reconciling herself to this
sudden and unexpected change in the arrange-
ment of her little household. She made many
objections, and almost tearfully besought Gustavus to remain yet a little longer under the
parental roof, and not so young to venture out
into a fearful and unknown world. She promised him every motherly care and attention,
and when she found that her representations

had no effect in changing her husband's or
Gustavus's resolution, she did her best to supply
her adopted son with all he could need for his
journey. She carefully mended and arranged
his under-garments, adding thereto from the
cloth woven for her own little ones. Gustavus
was deeply touched, and all the bitterness
which the memory of former ill treatment
occasionally woke in his soul vanished in the
gush of grateful tears which the sight of his
adopted mother's kindness drew from his eyes.

Time sped, and the hour of departure came
at last! All was in readiness; a passport had
been obtained from the proper authorities, and
the parting visits had all been made. At the
first break of dawn, Braun and Gustavus left
the cottage. The heart of the latter was full,
almost to bursting. He must now leave behind
him all the scenes of his childhood, not indeed
strewed with roses, yet enlivened by many a
happy hour. Every step recalled to his memory the various scenes and events of his innocent childhood. It was no wonder that his
eyes were filled with tears, and that not a word
was spoken as the father and son ascended the

hill dividing the secluded valley from the level country on the opposite side. They reached the summit just as the sun was rising.

"We must part here, my son," said Braun. "Look, how brightly and clearly the sun is rising! May the morning of thy new life promise as fair a day! I can no longer watch over thee, and can only accompany thee with my prayers and good wishes. But I give thee into the hands of one who is a tender and loving Father to all the children of earth. My son, keep God ever before thine eyes and in thy heart, and beware of evil. Suffer no sinful thought, word, or deed to stain the purity of thy soul. Mayest thou find all thou seekest! But should the world fail thee, remember that thou still hast a father, and a father's house. And now, farewell! God and his angels be ever with thee!"

Gustavus wept aloud, and throwing his arms round his father's neck, exclaimed: "Father, dear father! Thanks, a thousand thanks!"

His utterance was stifled by the violence of his emotion, and he could say no more. Braun gently disengaged himself from the boy's em-

brace. He, too, was deeply moved, and, turning away, walked thoughtfully homeward.

Gustavus was thus at length alone. Behind
him lay the narrow valley, with all its tender
memories of his childish days, while before
him a vast and unknown world stretched far
away toward the distant horizon. The feeling
of his loneliness, and the consciousness that
there was now no one to whom he could turn
for aid and counsel, painfully oppressed him.
He fell upon his knees, and gave vent to his
emotions in silent but fervent prayer.

But, most fortunately, he was not of a character long or weakly to yield to melancholy
thoughts. His youth, courage, and cheerful
disposition soon gained the victory over his
depression. His long-cherished wish was finally fulfilled, and he knew that, if he would
win the substance of the sweet dreams and
aspirations which had so mysteriously stirred
within his soul, he must tread steadily onward,
and reach the far blue distance now gleaming
in the brilliant morning light. He stretched
forth his arms as if in greeting toward the
plain, tightened the cord that bound his little

bundle, and trod swiftly and firmly over the
pathway that was to lead him to his unknown
destiny.

It was a lovely spring morning. Far above
him floated the thousand-voiced chorus of the
larks, the finches twittered in the groves, and
the first storks proudly stalked across the
grassy meadows. The country people were on
every side occupied in furrowing the land, and
sowing the golden seeds of the future harvest.
Everywhere appeared the signs of an active
and joyous life, of a thorough renovation of all
the powers of nature.

All this filled our young friend's heart with
unspeakable delight. With an eye ever open
to beauty of every kind, nature kept no secrets from him. Every flower told its own
tale, and every waving tree softly whispered its
gentle story in his listening ear. It is the pre-
rogative of the pure in heart, of those who
hearken to the voice of God within their souls,
to ever find in nature a dear and confidential
friend, a never-failing source of the purest and
most rapturous delight. All disquiet and every
sorrow must be soothed by the holy peace and

harmonious life which flow with the breath of
God through all the veins of creation. That
we so seldom find this consolation, this exalted
repose, must be the result of some fault in our-
selves ; our insatiable desires, our glowing
passions, our sins, step in between us and be-
neficent nature, so that we see only her out-
ward form, only the rude materials, while the
living, breathing spirit of God, sustaining and
glorifying the whole creation, escapes our view
and eludes our comprehension.

Gustavus was besides a born artist, that is
to say, he saw the whole creation in its manifold relations to the beautiful, and, as the pastor had said, everything, for him, at once
became a picture. His fancy was continually
occupied in grouping together the lovely forms
presented by external nature, or arising from
within, — the growth of his own imagination.
We cannot, then, wonder that he felt neither
the length of the way nor the dreariness of solitude. His steps were winged, and his countenance beamed with happy smiles. Who, among
the occupants of the comfortable vehicles from
time to time rolling past, would have thought

that that cheerful, smiling lad, without money, without friends, without prospects of any kind, impelled solely by the mysterious promptings of his own heart, was just entering a vast and unknown world, with the intention of conse-crating his life to an art of which he as yet knew but little more than the name, and of whose depths and difficulties he had not the faintest conception.

CHAPTER IV.

GUSTAVUS SEEKS A MASTER, AND FANCIES HIS
SEARCH SUCCESSFUL.

On the third day after his departure, Gustavus reached the capital. The buoyant hopes
which had sustained him during his journey
through the open country, with the free, blue
vault of heaven overhead, began to desert him
as he approached the place where the mystic
scroll of his future destiny was to be unrolled.
On every side beautiful dwellings, surrounded
by neat and tasteful gardens, met his view;
but to one accustomed to the freedom of the
hills, to the vast forms of the mountains, and
the shady recesses of the woods and vales, all
looked so narrow and confined! The turmoil
gradually increased, and the boy's heart beat
quicker and faster, until he finally found him-

self in the midst of the bustle and confusion
characterizing the more frequented parts of
most large cities.   Hundreds of pedestrians
came streaming toward him, and hundreds
more bore him onward with the living current.
Carriage after carriage rolled rapidly past,
while innumerable carts and loaded wagons
thundered heavily over the stones. His ears
were deafened by the ceaseless and bewildering
clatter. As he advanced, the streets became
narrower, the houses higher, and the throng
more dense. At every moment something
new, strange, and wonderful claimed his attention. He was especially astonished with the
profusion of objects hitherto unknown to him
displayed in the windows of the splendid
stores.

Without exactly knowing how, he finally
reached the market-place, in the very centre of
the city, where trade was most bustling and
active, and the display of wealth most dazzling.

There he stood, — poor Gustavus!

A feeling of utter loneliness and helplessness
stole over him. The busy citizens hastened
past, all occupied with their own affairs, talk-

ing and laughing together, or absorbed in the
consideration of some weighty speculation, and
not one had a word or even a glance of sympathy to bestow upon the friendless boy.

Whither should he turn ? How should he
begin ? For the first time did he tremble at
the thought of having ventured alone and without a guide into the whirl and tumult of the
outer world. A course which, afar off in the
primitive simplicity of a rural district, had
seemed to him perfectly easy and natural, now
assumed the aspect of a gigantic undertaking,
beyond the remotest bounds of possibility.
Where was he to look for a master to instruct
him in the art of painting ? And when found,
how could he hope that an entire stranger
would take any interest in an unknown boy ?
In vain did he endeavor to ask a single question of any member of the motley throng hasten-
ing past : the words died upon his lips. Oppressed by the weight of these new thoughts
and impressions, exhausted in body and mind,
he sank upon the steps of the court-house.
His heart was sorely troubled. He thought of
his home, of the green hills, of the peaceful

cottage in the wood, of his good father, and of
his dear little brothers and sisters! He longed
for wings to fly away and see them all once
more. These melancholy thoughts and dear
remembrances finally overcame him, and he
burst into an agony of tears.

He sat thus, until the increasing darkness
warned him of the necessity of seeking some
shelter for the night. He at once compre-
hended that the stately mansions for travellers,
which he had passed on his way to the market-
place, were no abodes for him; and, retracing
his steps, he finally stopped at an inn in one
of the suburbs, purporting to offer rest and
food to wagoners and country people. Here,
after partaking of a scanty meal, he flung
himself upon a straw-bed, and soon, in a long
and heavy sleep, forgot all his cares and sorrows.

The following morning, he awoke with a
lighter heart and renewed courage. His position seemed to him less hopeless. He had as
yet made no effort to attain his end; how, then,
could he already feel like despairing? He
went very early into the city, and the pure rays

of the morning sun threw quite a new light
upon its busy streets and lofty edifices. His
love of beauty was at once captivated by the
palatial dwellings adorning even the suburbs.

From the lofty towers resounded the deep-
toned bells, calling the faithful to prayer. The
churches are in every land the only buildings
which hospitably open their doors to all without exception, to the rich and the poor, to the
happy and the miserable. Gustavus soon
found himself within a lofty church, and a new
world of wonders was here presented to his
astonished senses.

How boldly rose the majestic arch roofing
the main aisle, how gracefully towered the
two rows of mighty columns, and how the
altar in the far perspective glittered with its
gilded carvings, its paintings, and its statues;
how gloriously broke the light of morning
through the narrow but lofty stained-glass
windows! Of such paintings as covered the
walls and adorned the altar Gustavus had
never even dreamed. What noble forms!
What expression in the countenances! What
glorious coloring!

Intoxicated with delight, Gustavus hastened from one to another, and finally seated
himself before one which had excited his especial admiration. It was a Christ in the garden of Gethsemane. The divine form seemed
quivering 'neath the anguish of the moment,
and the prayer, "Father, if it be thy will,
remove this cup from me," seemed struggling
on the lips. High overhead the heavens were
opened, and an angel, bearing in his right hand
the inevitable cross, seemed about descending.
The light streaming from above fell full upon
the Saviour, while the remainder of the picture was enveloped in darkness. Below lay
the sleeping figures of the three disciples, — the
mild John, the fiery Peter, and the wise and
earnest James. The profound quiet and repose
characterizing the attitudes of the sleepers presented a most striking contrast to the agony of
spirit, the holy suffering, expressed in every
lineament of their Master's countenance.

Gustavus was spell-bound, and thought he
could never weary of gazing on that picture;
and when at length the full tones of the organ
announced the commencement of the service,

the boy's head sank in prayer; past, present, and future seemed to pass away from his mind; he felt only joy and devotion; all his doubts and uncertainties had vanished, and when he arose, he felt strengthened for the combat of life, and interpenetrated with fervent gratitude to the great Creator, who had not only permitted him to enjoy his works in the realm of nature, but had now revealed to him the lofty things that were to be accomplished by genius and a pure inspiration in the realm of art.

The service was over; the throng dispersed; Gustavus alone remained in the church; nor did he think of departing until the sacristan aroused him from his reverie by reminding him of the necessity of closing the doors. The boy hastened out into the street. Consoled and strengthened by the short commune with truth, beauty, and divine love which had been vouchsafed him in the temple, he felt his hopes revive, and he determined at once to pursue the object of his search. During the course of that day he learned the names and addresses of three painters, but all his efforts seemed to bring him no nearer to his goal. The first was not at home, the second refused to see him, and the third, after listening to his little history, declined rendering him any assistance, and, with a shrug of the shoulders, bade him depart.

Even this experience, however, could not utterly destroy the boy's confidence. He thought, If I do not succeed to-day, I may, perhaps, to-morrow. But that happy morrow seemed in no haste to dawn upon our hero; four days had already elapsed since his first arrival in the city, the little fund with which his father had supplied him was nearly exhausted, and yet he was no nearer to the fulfilment of his hopes than when he had first entered the capital.

Vain plans and fruitless efforts occupied the weary hours. Gustavus became very anxious, and at length almost despaired. The church was the only place where he found consolation and repose.

One day, when most dispirited and downhearted, he seated himself upon a bench by the wayside. His little portfolio lay at his feet. Even this treasure no longer afforded him any pleasure. During the few days just past he had seen so much that was grand and beautiful, that his own attempts appeared to him utterly worthless. He had begun to entertain serious doubts of his own ability and vocation.

His attention, however, being suddenly attracted by a group of trees which struck him as unusually beautiful and picturesque, he drew forth a sheet of paper and commenced a sketch. While thus occupied, a stranger came and seated himself upon a neighboring bench, whence he watched the progress of the boy's work. After a few moments of silent observation, he addressed Gustavus, saying, —

"You are making a charming picture. Will you let me see it?"

Gustavus placed the drawing in the stranger's hand.

"Indeed," continued the latter, "this shows considerable skill. You probably belong to one of our city schools!"

"O no! I do not live here."

"Well! you must at least have studied in a good school. You depict nature to the very life. From whom have you learned?"

"From myself. I never had a master."

"That is really astonishing. Whence come you, and who are your parents?"

Gustavus replied briefly but candidly, without, however, mentioning the cause of his journey to the city, or his present gloomy prospects.

"But what do you intend to do in this city?" asked the stranger.

"I intend to be a painter. Of course I could not pursue my studies in the village, and with my father's permission I came to Breslau in search of a master."

"Have you the necessary means?"

"Ah no!" said Gustavus with a blush; "I have only a few pennies."

"But you have letters of introduction?"

"No, indeed! I have not a single acquaintance in Breslau."

"And how, then, do you expect to attain your purpose of learning the art of painting?"

"I hoped to find some master whom my entreaties might move to take me as his pupil."

The stranger laughed, but soon assuming a serious aspect, continued, —

"My young friend, you are evidently very ignorant of the ways of the world, neither does your father seem to be much more experienced; otherwise you would both have seen the impracticability of your present course."

"But what can I do, now that I have taken this step?" cried Gustavus, his eyes filling with tears.

The stranger made no reply, but, as if lost in thought, turned over the leaves of the little portfolio which Gustavus had willingly submitted to his inspection. One most deeply versed in the knowledge of mankind would have been puzzled in divining the purposes and intentions concealed by the stranger's cold and impassive countenance. He suddenly interrupted his apparently profound meditation by saying, —

"Can you write? I mean, do you write a good hand?"

"I think so. My master considered me his best scholar."

"Will you give me a specimen?"

Gustavus wrote a few lines in a clear and beautiful hand.

" That is, indeed, very well done. It may prove useful."

The stranger again seemed absorbed in thought. Gustavus, meanwhile, had time to observe him more closely. He was a well-dressed, middle-aged man. His face was pale and deeply wrinkled, his eyes brilliant, but overshadowed by heavy brows. Had Gustavus been more conversant with the various types of humanity, he would have mistrusted that face and eye. Of course no such idea presented itself to his mind, and he was only too happy to be thus sympathizingly noticed by a stranger.

After a somewhat lengthy pause, the unknown again resumed, —

" I am sorry for you, my young friend; your simplicity and inexperience have placed you in a very awkward position. But take courage; fate may yet be propitious. A happy accident has thrown in your way all that you sought in vain. I am a painter ! "

" You a painter ? " cried Gustavus, joyfully springing to his feet and seizing the stranger's hand.

"Yes, I am a painter, and one by no means unknown to fame. My pictures adorn all our exhibitions. Did you never hear of the celebrated Feldberg?"

Gustavus blushed as he confessed his ignorance. "Ah! I forgot you were from the country. Of course you never heard of me there. I feel deeply interested in your fate. You are endowed with unmistakable talent!"

The boy's frame quivered with the excess of delight which these words occasioned in his soul.

"I will take you as my pupil," continued the stranger; "that is, if you are willing."

"If I am willing!" cried Gustavus, casting a grateful glance toward heaven.

"You may then begin with me; there is a place open for you. You are poor; I ask no pay, and you will eat at my own table."

"O thou almighty God!" cried Gustavus, "how have I deserved this blessing?"

The boy's delight was so boundless and inexpressible, that he could scarcely refrain from flinging himself at the stranger's feet.

"Come, child, moderate your rapture. Now

if you are to be my pupil without my exact-
ing from you the slightest compensation, you
will readily comprehend that I have a right
to make a few conditions."

"I will joyfully do all you can ask of me!"

"The first condition is, that you punctually
and unhesitatingly accomplish all that I set
before you to do. Will you promise me?"

"Yes, indeed, most willingly!"

"The second is, that you ask no questions
concerning any task I may require you to ex-
cute. Will you also agree to that?"

"I will," replied Gustavus.

"Well, then, the third and last is, that you
must be very industrious! You will have
but little time at your own disposal, and hence
it will be best for you to leave the house as
seldom as possible. If you think you will not
find the confinement irksome, our bargain is
concluded."

Gustavus found no fault with this condition,
and readily acquiesced.

"Give me your hand then," said the stranger. "Now we mutually understand each
other."

Had Gustavus been less absorbed in the excess of his own delight, he might perhaps have
observed the cunning and mysterious smile
which flitted athwart the stranger's hard features as the boy confidingly placed his little
hand in the offered clasp.

" Now, my lad, we will go for your clothes,
and then you will accompany me home."

They went. The boy's face was radiant
with joy, and his step lighter than it had been
for many a weary day. Poor lad! He little
thought he had contracted an engagement
threatening the most fearful consequences.
Let us not wonder at his simplicity, for of
evil he barely knew more than the name,
and he had hitherto met with no bad men.
He had never heard of those specious evil-
doers who lurk in the by-ways of great cities,
pursuing all kinds of infamous avocations, and
ever ready to ensnare the young and inexperienced. His noble and affectionate heart lay
trustingly open to his fellow-mortals, and how
could he suspect the first man who had offered
him consolation in his almost hopeless condition, by speaking words of sympathy, and by,

moreover, offering to aid him in the fulfilment
of his dearest wishes? He had no thought
beyond his present happiness. The "celebrated" painter seemed to him a messenger
from heaven, sent especially to deliver him
from all his troubles. Even the strange conditions imposed upon him by his new friend
excited no suspicion. They seemed to him
so perfectly natural, so precisely what a master
had a right to demand from his pupil, that
he accepted them without a moment's hesitation.

Gustavus followed his new master through
numberless streets and alleys, until they finally
reached a distant quarter of the city, and
stopped before a tall, narrow house, with a
peaked roof, and walls blackened by time.
Although it was still early in the day, the
house-door was already locked, and not until
after repeated ringing and knocking was it
finally opened by a hideous old woman in a
dirty gown. The dame cast an astonished
glance at the boy.

"This is my pupil!" said Feldberg. "He
is to live with us. I hope you will like each
other."

So saying, he led Gustavus up three flights of narrow stairs, and, opening a door at the head of the last flight, entered a large but sombre looking apartment.

"Soh! Now we are at home, you must make yourself quite comfortable, my lad!"

In accordance with this invitation, Gustavus laid his bundle in a corner, and silently seated himself, while his master walked up and down the room. The boy gazed round his new abode. On the walls hung a few insignificant pictures; while here and there were scattered some of the utensils employed in painting. Disorder reigned paramount, and not a trace was to be seen of the artistic grace which Gustavus had fancied must be found in the studio of a great painter. His delight was somewhat diminished, and his heart began to be troubled with sundry doubts and misgivings.

The evening passed, however, without any further cause for anxiety. The scanty remains of the evening meal were set before the boy, and as he was very hungry, he devoured the unsavory viands with considerable appetite.

After supper, Feldberg showed Gustavus to an attic-room, where a miserable pallet had been prepared for him. When alone, he made a close examination of his apartment, and his comfort was certainly not increased by the discovery that the door of the chamber was locked on the outside.

CHAPTER V.

AND who, then, was this Mr. Feldberg? He
was in fact a painter; at least, he thus styled
himself, and was thus considered among his
neighbors. But, either through indolence or
want of success, he had not actually practised
his art for many years, and had devoted himself to pursuits more in accordance with the
restlessness of his temperament, and proffering
more ample remuneration. We cannot spe-
cify his occupations, as they were numerous, of
divers characters, and most carefully hidden
from the public view. Generally speaking, he
was a kind of universal agent, such as we find
in most large cities; that is, he was ready to
engage in any business promising profit, great
or small. He negotiated sales, lent money at
high rates, and proffered assistance to all who

had fallen into embarrassment of any kind, —
his aid, however, usually causing the total ruin
of those who were unfortunate enough to
seek it.

We cannot say he was governed by any very
lofty conceptions of duty or of the claims of
conscience. His ruling principle seemed to
be, All is allowable that fills the purse. He
could wring the last penny, — ay, the very
heart's blood from the miserable creatures who
had fallen into his power. Were we to call
him a thief and a swindler, we should be
guilty of no slander; but he was so skilful in
concealing his misdeeds, or in masking them
with an appearance of legality, that, although
he had on several occasions been cited to appear before the public tribunals, he had always
escaped condemnation.

But our readers may ask, Why had this
plausible scoundrel thus entrapped our friend
Gustavus? Of course he had not acted without a sufficient motive, and his customary cunning and duplicity had guided his decision in
this case, as in all others in which his interests
were concerned.

His speculations frequently required close imitations of various handwritings, for he was so accustomed to false dealing of every kind, that he did not hesitate a moment at counterfeiting a name, or even an entire document. His own ready and practised hand had hitherto been all sufficient for the execution of his projects; but that guilty member had recently become unsteady, and he could no longer rely upon its tremulous aid. Accident threw Gustavus in his way, and he at once recognized in the friendless boy the tool he needed. The lad's skill in drawing and writing, especially if developed and perfected to this especial end, would entirely satisfy all his requisitions. He also rejoiced in the boy's simplicity and utter want of experience. Nothing seemed more easy than gradually to enclose him in so intricate a net that escape would be impossible, and if he could be induced to commit one actual misdeed, the wary schemer knew that his empire would be for ever secured. He fully relied upon the truth of a saying propounded by one of our most celebrated authors: " Give the devil a single hair, and you are his for all eternity ! "

Feldberg's plans extended a long way into the future, and covered a wide field of action. He had once counterfeited certain bank-bills, and had attempted to circulate the false paper through the city. The fraud, however, was discovered, and suspicion had fallen upon him; but he lied so stoutly, and it was found so impossible to prove anything against him, that he was released without having received the due reward of his misdeeds. Since then he had not dared to renew that branch of his nefarious transactions. But Gustavus's extraordinary ability now seemed to afford him the means of returning to his old tricks with a surer prospect of success, and he could almost feel within his covetous grasp the treasures thence flowing into his coffers.

Gustavus had then fallen into the most dangerous hands, and yet the poor boy suspected nothing. He slept in his garret, on his hard bed, and his peaceful slumbers were sweetened by the loveliest and most alluring dreams. Glorious paintings, the work of his own hands, stood round him; a noble and beautiful lady — the same whose portrait he possessed in the

locket — floated toward him from some unknown region of light and bliss, and fondly
pressed him to her heart. But when the
morning came and he awoke, these lovely
visions vanished, and nothing remained to him
but four bare walls.

His first thought, however, was one of gratitude that he had been so providentially led to
so secure a shelter. He promised himself to
bear with cheerfulness every privation, if he
could only in the end attain the accomplish-
ment of his dearest wishes.

His master brought him his breakfast, and
when the simple meal was over, said, "Now,
my lad, we must go to work! As a learner,
you must for the present expect nothing but
school exercises. In the art of painting you
will require the greatest nicety of touch and
execution. Hence you must learn to copy
neatly. Here are two sheets, on one of which
is traced a variety of strange figures. The
lines cross each other in every direction, and
seem without meaning or purpose; but you will
find this a most useful exercise, as you must
copy the figures so exactly that no one could

tell the copy from the original. On the other
sheet you will find an extract from a manu-
script written in no very elegant hand, but I
assure you it will prove useful, as in copying it
precisely you will attain greater exactitude.
Not a single stroke or dot must be omitted,
and you must especially apply yourself to the
mastering of the general character of the hand-
writing. And now I hope you will be diligent
and attentive, that when I return at noon I
may have reason to rejoice in your progress."

Feldberg left the room, locking the door behind him. Gustavus immediately sat down to
his task, which did not strike him as in any
way peculiar. He knew that without exactitude it would be impossible to succeed in por-
traying a house or a tree, to say nothing of the
delicate lines of a human countenance. He
determined to progress as rapidly as practica-
ble in these elementary studies, that he might
the sooner attain to the more attractive por-
tions of his chosen art.

The boy's nimble fingers soon completed the
first portion of his task to his own entire satisfaction, and he hoped, to that of his master.

At noon, the latter came, praised some parts, blamed others, and incited his pupil to still closer exactitude.

Day after day passed in the same manner. Nothing was proposed but the endless copying of utterly senseless figures, gradually becoming more and more complicated, or the imitating of an infinite variety of handwritings. Our Gustavus was finally seized with an insurmountable repugnance to this soulless, yet most wearisome labor. There was, however, no way of freeing himself from the thraldom of his master, who continued to require the daily practice of similar exercises until the boy should have attained the requisite exactitude.

Gustavus had on one occasion ventured to beg for some new species of task, but a threatening glance from the master's eye, and a hasty oath from his lips, soon silenced the modest petition. Since that hour, Gustavus had begun to fear Feldberg. He trembled when he heard his step upon the stairway, and always felt uneasy in his presence. The boy's pure soul began to divine the vicinity of an unholy and wicked spirit. As yet, however, Gus-

tavus had no very clear impressions with
regard to his actual position, and was too weak
to contend with his master. Inwardly sigh-
ing, yet endeavoring to do his best, he was
continually forced to renew his hated labor.

This, however, was not his only source of
suffering. He was a child of the mountains.
He had always been accustomed to the fresh
air and freedom of the country ; his days had
been passed amid breezy hills, smiling vales,
and luxuriant forests, and now he was confined
between four bare walls, and constantly forced
to breathe the same close and unwholesome
atmosphere. What a melancholy change !

His master did not allow him a single moment of freedom. For many days he had not
seen the blue of heaven except through the
dingy panes of the parlor windows, or through
the tiny opening in his garret room. He
began to suffer from an irrepressible feeling of
home-sickness. When, in the early morning,
or the evening twilight, he looked forth from
his lofty station into the far distance, his longing was unutterable. He envied the swallows
fluttering and twittering in the free, pure air

around his lonely prison; and the lot of a chimney-sweep, whom he heard singing from the top of a neighboring chimney, seemed to him inexpressibly delightful. Far away, beyond the most distant roofs, he saw the waving tree-tops, and the blue outline of a distant mountain chain. He longed for the wings of the doves, that he might fly far, far away!

O, if he could only once more rest in the cool shade of the forest, only once more breathe the fresh air of the mountains! No felicity seemed to him comparable to the fulfilment of this desire. And then, too, he thought of all his dear ones at home. He fancied himself seated at his father's feet, fondly gazing upon his smiling and friendly countenance, or surrounded by the lively band of his young brothers and sisters, or again playing in the meadow by the brook, with his school companions.

Poor boy! He felt he could not long endure the pain of separation from all that had made life dear to him. He strove in vain to love a master who treated him alternately with a sort of repulsive kindliness, and the most terrifying harshness. The truth that he had

been taken into the house from no benevolent
motive, but for some selfish, perhaps wicked,
purpose, gradually began to dawn upon his
mind.   The old housekeeper, also, had never a
kind word to bestow on him, being always very
cross, and watching him even more closely than
his master.

Yet, even in this melancholy situation, Gustavus had two sources of consolation: his trust
in God, and the dear image in the locket.
Through an instinctive caution he had concealed this treasure from his master, and had
refrained from mentioning the mystery enshrouding his birth.   Only when alone would
he take the picture from his bosom and gaze
long and earnestly into the beautiful countenance.   He felt quite sure that it was indeed
his mother's portrait.   All his words were now
addressed to her; she held a place in all his
thoughts and feelings.   The longer he gazed
upon the picture, the more life-like it became
to him: the gentle eyes seemed actually filled
with love, and the lips almost ready to speak
words of consolation and encouragement, — *to
whisper of happy days yet to come.*   The dear

image haunted his dreams; under many aspects and amid a variety of circumstances, but always mild and loving, it hovered round him; now walking with him through some charming landscape, now supporting his weary head upon its bosom, and again, rejoicing with him over some beautiful picture in which he had succeeded to his heart's content. When he awoke, the memory of these dreams filled his soul with mingled pain and rapture.

Thus passed several weeks. The boy's position became more and more unendurable, for the vague suspicion he had begun to entertain with regard to Feldberg increased to a painful degree. His uneasiness was by no means diminished by the conversation we are about to relate. One evening, Feldberg came home in an excellent humor; he had probably been successful in some rascally enterprise. Calling the boy to his side, he said, —

"Gustavus, my lad, I am very well satisfied with you. During the past few days you have performed your tasks so well that I must soon declare you quite perfect. Your copies are so excellent, that even my experienced eye can scarcely distinguish them from the originals."

"If that be indeed so," said Gustavus, timidly, "may I not hope that you will now give me some other kind of exercises?"

"What kind of exercises do you want?"

"Heads, landscapes, flowers,—what you will!"

"Do you then really wish to be a painter?"

Gustavus opened his eyes, but ventured no reply to this question.

"O yes, I know you have a fancy that way. You think you have been gifted with a marvellous talent for painting. But what if I were to tell you that you have no talent at all?"

"That would indeed be horrible!" stammered Gustavus.

"No, not the faintest, I am quite sure. You have no fancy, no invention. You can never be more than a mere copyist."

The boy's eyes filled with tears.

"Come, don't cry, my lad! I will trust you with a secret. Your extraordinary skill in copying is worth a great deal more to you than the loftiest talent with which you could have been endowed."

Gustavus gazed speechless into his master's face.

"Do you not know that many a writing is worth more than a thousand dollars; and who now-a-days will pay a thousand dollars for a picture?"

"How can that be possible?" replied Gustavus, blushing deeply.

"It is true, you little simpleton, although you cannot as yet comprehend it. But you will learn in time. If you are industrious, obedient, and secret, I will one day teach you how to become a very rich man."

Gustavus sprang to his feet, and cried,—

"O, my good master, I do not care to learn that! I had hoped you would teach me painting; but as you say I have no talent, I suppose I never could become an artist, and consequently am of no use here. Let me go away, I beseech you!"

"You fool!" said Feldberg; "that is quite impossible. Do you think that I have taught and fed you during four weeks all for nothing?"

The boy fell at the man's feet and embraced his knees.

"Let me go, I beseech you, for God's sake!

I am good for nothing, — nothing at all!
Ah! indeed I must leave this place!"

"Silence!" thundered Feldberg; "you will
stay here, — you *must* stay here! Do you
hear?"

These words were spoken in so fearful a tone,
and accompanied by so fierce a glance, that
Gustavus shrank back in terror. Almost me-
chanically did he obey the command to betake
himself to his own chamber.

When alone, he found his mind in a terrible
state of confusion. Strange thoughts and feelings flitted athwart his brain, but he strove in
vain to reduce them to order. By degrees he
became calmer. Although utterly inexperienced in the ways of the world, he possessed a
clear intellect, and an upright judgment. The
preceding conversation had thrown a fearful
light upon his present situation. No, thought
he, this man is no painter! But what is he?
Why has he lured me hither? What does he
want with me? Wherefore this eternal copying of senseless figures and handwritings?

An almost forgotten memory flashed across
his mind. His teacher had once told him that

there were persons who made a business of falsifying and counterfeiting notes and documents. What if Feldberg were such a man? Horrible! And what if he intended to employ him as a tool! At this thought his blood stiffened in his veins; he was stricken in his most sensitive point! A profound sense of right, and an incorruptible feeling of honor, were among his most prominent characteristics.

Wherefore, thought he, this confinement, this careful locking of my door, and this anxiety lest I should hold any communication with my fellow-beings? Is he afraid I will betray him before he has made sure of me? Wherefore these secret visits, at which I am never permitted to be present, — this dark and mysterious mode of life,— this anxiety to avoid all observation? The more Gustavus reflected, the more sure he became that he had fallen into the hands of a villain.

He threw himself upon his knees and prayed: " O my God! save me from the snares of the wicked. Let me die, if it be Thy will, but keep my heart and my hand from evil! "

It was very late that night when he sank into an uneasy sleep, disturbed by fearful dreams.

The following day, when Feldberg called Gustavus to leave his chamber and come down to him, the wily master was apparently more friendly than ever.

"My lad," said he, "you acted yesterday like a little fool, and you must have seen that you cannot trifle with me. I hope you have learned a good lesson for the future. Our interests are now closely entwined, and the better friends we are, the more advantageous for you. I have an exercise for you with which you cannot fail to be pleased. Here is a neat little picture on which are stamped the Prussian eagle and the Prussian arms, with sundry other pretty figures. All these must be copied; but mind you, exactly, so that no one could tell the copy from the original. Do you hear? If you succeed to my satisfaction, you may rely upon a large reward."

When Feldberg had left the house, — for he was always absent during the greater part of the day, — Gustavus examined the paper which had been placed before him. It was a Prussian treasury note. He remembered having seen similar papers in his father's hands, but he had then paid no regard to their meaning. Now when among other words he found these two, — "Five Dollars," — he began to suspect that this note might be employed to represent an equivalent in money. And he was expected to copy that! To what end? While, with a beating heart, he was anxiously considering the matter, his eyes fell upon a line of fine writing running around the rim of the note. He read as follows : —

"According to the law of the land, whoever counterfeits, or causes to be counterfeited, treasury notes, whoever circulates said counterfeits, or aids and abets their circulation, incurs the penalty of a fine equal to tenfold the value of the counterfeited note or notes, together with severe corporeal punishment and imprisonment, the term of which imprisonment may be extended to the duration of the natural life, with hard labor."

We cannot describe the horror with which Gustavus read these words. All was now perfectly clear! And was he then to become a counterfeiter, — a criminal? To load his conscience with a heavy weight of guilt, and to render himself liable to the severest punishments of the law? He trembled from head to foot, as if he had already committed the evil deed. His first thought was flight; but he found all the doors, as usual, locked.

"I must escape," cried he; "I must fly from this den of wickedness, even if I am forced to leap from the windows!"

He sank down in one corner and wept bitterly.

"Ah, my father!" sighed he, "if you only knew the fearful abyss which yawns before me, you would fly to the aid of your own Gustavus!"

The paper, still lying on the table, inspired him with indescribable horror. "No, not one stroke will I make; I will have my hand cut off before I use it for any wicked purpose!" He sprang to his feet. "What right has this man to plunge me into temporal and eternal ruin? He may beat me, he may lock me up, but he shall not stain my soul. For the preservation of its purity, I am accountable both to myself and to my God!"

Thus, amid conflicting feelings, fluctuating between hopeless despair and courageous resolution, Gustavus passed the long hours of that fearful morning. At noon, Feldberg returned.

"Well, my lad," cried he, "have you been diligent? How much have you done? What does this mean?" continued he, his eye falling upon the blank sheet still lying where he had left it. "Have you done nothing?"

"I have done nothing," replied Gustavus, in a resolute, although somewhat tremulous tone.

"And why not, may I ask?"

"I read upon that paper that whoever copies it is a criminal and liable to severe punishment."

Feldberg laughed aloud. "Is that all? You little fool! Who says that this copy is to be circulated? It is only intended as an exercise for you."

"I shudder at the very idea of such exercises."

"Then you will not copy the paper?"

"No, not that one."

Feldberg's face assumed a fearful expression; his hands quivered convulsively; he fastened his eye on Gustavus, like a serpent on the poor bird destined to be its next victim. The boy's courage, however, rose with the actual presence of danger.

"Master," said he, "you brought me here under a promise to teach me painting, but I see that if I remain with you I shall never become a painter. You had better, then, suffer me to depart."

"And what do you think you will become if you remain with me?" asked Feldberg, his voice trembling with rage.

"I must say it!" cried Gustavus. "I have no earthly possession except a guiltless conscience, — shall I lose that, and become a cheat and a counterfeiter?"

The outburst of rage which followed this speech was indeed terrific; Feldberg seized the boy, flung him to the ground, and seemed about to strangle him.

"But no," he suddenly cried, "we have other means of subduing you. Off with you, to your room!"

He half dragged the boy up the steep stairs, and pushing him into his room, locked the door on the outside.

The day passed, and no dinner came. Is it hunger that is to subdue me? thought Gustavus. A cold shudder ran through all his veins.

He felt he must escape. The idea of flight became more and more fixed in his mind. His life, and more, his eternal salvation, were at stake. But how? — He looked forth from his little window; a giddy depth lay below, and the neighboring roofs were too distant to afford him any aid.

The only possible mode of escape was by the stairway, but then the door was locked. Long and vainly did he ponder; no way of forcing it open presented itself to his mind, until suddenly his eye chanced to fall upon a large nail, only partially driven into the wall. His heart leaped with joy! His efforts to withdraw it proved successful. How if he were to bend the point and use its as a key? The lock seemed a very simple one, — or perhaps he might use it as a pry to force back the bolt.

8 *

He made an attempt, the bolt began to move, and he now felt quite sure that he could open the door. But he must wait until after nightfall, for the housekeeper, who was always to be found in the kitchen, watched the steps with argus eyes. And when fairly down stairs, how was he to get through the hall door? He determined to hide in the lower story until the morning, when the door would be opened, and then slip out. After much deliberation, Gustavus finally decided upon adopting this plan.

The evening passed, and no supper. I am right, he intends to ruin me! thought Gustavus. The effort must be made, and midnight seemed to him the best time for beginning his operations.

Our young readers may imagine how endless the intermediate hours of anxious delay seemed to the poor boy.

CHAPTER VI.

FLIGHT AND DELIVERANCE.

THE bells from the towers announced the hour of midnight. Now is the time, thought Gustavus. He packed his little wallet, tied up his portfolio, and then recommended himself to the protection of his Heavenly Father. This done, he went to the door and listened; all was silent as the grave. He softly inserted the nail into the open crack, — his forehead was covered with a cold sweat, — the bolt gave way, and the door was unfastened. Unspeakable was the delight thrilling every member of his youthful frame.

He crossed the threshold and carefully re-bolted the door. Scarcely daring to breathe, he felt his way on tip-toe down stairs. The most profound silence and impenetrable dark-

ness pervaded the house. The beating of his
own heart was the only sound he heard. He
stopped a moment on the landing outside of
Feldberg's door; from the back room where
the housekeeper slept proceeded a terrible
snoring, which made him feel quite secure as
far as she was concerned. He then descended
the two remaining flights at a somewhat more
rapid pace.

Scarcely had he reached the ground floor,
when he was startled by a sudden noise. A
key was placed from without in the lock of the
house-door. Gustavus shivered, and barely
retained presence of mind sufficient to hide
behind some barrels under the stairway. Horror stricken, he recognized his master's voice.
Feldberg entered, accompanied by another
man; but the boy's delight may be imagined
when he heard that dreaded voice say, "I will
leave the door unlocked, as you will not have
long to stay; our business will soon be finished." Gustavus waited until the last echo
of the retreating footsteps had died away,
when, emerging from his hiding-place, he
flung open the heavy door and rushed out into
the street.

No human pen could describe his feelings. No shipwrecked mariner, whom the mercy of God had just snatched from all the horrors of a watery grave, could feel more grateful or enraptured than did our Gustavus, when he had fairly left his tormentor's den behind him. He seemed like one intoxicated with delight. The street lamps shed but a glimmering light, but the stars of heaven shone above his head; and he enjoyed to the full extent the privilege of choosing his own way and directing his own footsteps. He felt as if just awakened from some long and fearful dream, as if suddenly restored from some shadowy land of phantoms to the living and breathing realities of life. He walked for hours without a thought of fatigue, and finally reached the outskirts of the city, where the fresh country air blowing upon his face rendered him doubly happy. The vast city sleeping at his feet failed to excite a single emotion of apprehension; he was scarcely aware of its existence. He felt himself alone with his God, and his soul poured itself forth in the most fervent and joyful thanksgiving.

The intensity of his delight, however, began

to abate, when, with the dawn, came a shivering
feeling of cold and a gnawing sensation of hunger, for it had been nearly four-and-twenty
hours since the poor boy had tasted a mouth-
ful. These physical requirements recalled him
to a sense of his desolate and friendless condition. Human life began to stir abroad.
The country people commenced driving their
well-laden carts and wagons into the populous
town, and Gustavus soon found himself surrounded by all the bustle of the approaching
market hour. With a penny or so still remaining from his little store, he satisfied his hunger
at a baker's, and then began to consider what
he had better do next.

His first thought was to return to his father.
" But no," said he to himself; " I asked my
father for a year's trial, and it would be cow-
ardly to abandon all my hopes and projects
before six weeks had fairly passed."

His self-esteem and self-reliance, together
with an unconquerable love for his chosen art,
—a love which not even the misery of his last
experience could extinguish,—revived. Ah!
thought he, if I only knew some one who could

advise me, and show me some way of relieving myself from my present state of doubt and embarrassment!

His thoughts suddenly fell upon the kind pastor of the village church. He felt that, could he only see him, he would receive both counsel and substantial aid. This idea at once gave rise to another.

"How?" he cried, "are there not plenty of clergymen in this great city, and would any one of them repulse me after learning all my troubles and misfortunes? Are they not all servants of Him who called the burdened and heavy-laden to himself? How could they fail to pity a poor lad who asks nothing from them but a little consolation, and some good counsel to guide his steps amid the labyrinth of life."

Encouraged by this consideration, he went toward one of the large churches, and was delighted at finding a house near by, the door-plate of which announced the residence of a clergyman. He rang, was admitted, and soon stood before a venerable man who in the kindest manner asked him what he wanted. Gustavus, at first somewhat timidly, but gradually gaining confidence as he proceeded, related his whole story; who he was and whence he came, what had brought him to the capital, and all that had happened to him since his arrival.

The pastor listened attentively. He was pleased with the truthful expression of the boy's handsome countenance, and felt fully inclined to believe a tale so unreservedly, yet modestly related. He placed confidence in the poor boy, whose helpless and forlorn condition could not fail to excite a good man's compassion.

"My son," said he, "your simplicity and inexperience have led you into a most dangerous situation. Thank God, who has preserved you! You ask me what you had better do now. Of that we will speak hereafter. But we have first a most necessary work to accomplish. From all you have told me, this painter, Feldberg, must be a great villain, and who can tell how many of his evil deeds may still be lurking 'neath the veil of secrecy? It is now our duty to inform the city authorities of all we know."

Gustavus started! He had not thought of

this. The idea of standing before the magistracy, whom he had always fancied surrounded by the most awe-inspiring attributes of power and majesty, made him tremble from head to foot.

"Do not fear, my dear boy," said the pastor; "if you are innocent, you have no reason to be afraid. The magistracy does not indeed bear the sword in vain, but is only to be feared by the guilty. Who knows if God may not have chosen you as the instrument of delivering the community from one of its most dangerous members?"

The clergyman went with Gustavus to one of the chiefs of the police whom he knew very well. The mention of Feldberg's name, at the commencement of his narration, at once roused the attention of the police officer, who exclaimed,—

"Feldberg? The painter Feldberg? That indeed interests me! We have long suspected that man, and have only been waiting for some certain proof to punish him as he deserves. Pray, continue!"

The clergyman related all that he had heard

from Gustavus. The officer then asked the boy many questions, which he answered without hesitation, and apparently to the satisfaction of the official, who at the close of the examination said, —

" I thank you, reverend sir, that you have not shunned interfering in this unpleasant affair. You have rendered an invaluable service to all whom this villain's schemes might have plunged into ruin. The boy's deposition is quite sufficient to justify an immediate arrest. I must also detain the boy. 1 hope indeed that he is innocent; but until that is proved beyond a doubt, I cannot permit him to depart; the more, as it is necessary he should appear as a witness against the accused."

Gustavus was thunder-stricken. Again in captivity ! His face was pale as death, and all his limbs trembled.

" Mercy ! pity ! " cried he, wringing his hands. " I am innocent ! As true as there is a God in heaven, I have done nothing wrong ! "

The clergyman, who sincerely sympathized with the boy's distress, said a few kind words

in his behalf; but he was soon convinced that
the officer could not for the present spare him.
Both then strove with gentle words to reassure
the trembling child, and succeeded so well that
Gustavus with tolerable composure followed
the policeman (who had meanwhile been
called) into a very comfortable and by no
means terrifying place of detention.

We will now return to the gloomy house
from which Gustavus had so happily escaped.
Feldberg, little dreaming that his prisoner stood
trembling within three paces of him, went up
stairs with his companion. A short conversation then ensued, which, judging from the
whispered tones in which it was held, certainly
related to some villanous transaction. Soon
after, the stranger departed. Feldberg then
locked and bolted the doors. As he again
ascended the staircase, he thought of listening
a moment at the boy's door. All was quiet.
The lad must sleep well, thought he. Hunger
has not yet done its work !

As he found the door locked, he calmly returned to his own chamber. In the morning
he listened again. Again all was quiet. This

seemed incomprehensible, and he softly opened
the door; the room was empty. Our young
readers may imagine Feldberg's speechless
astonishment. His first thought was, that
Gustavus in despair had flung himself from the
window; and, hardened as he was, a cold shudder ran through all his limbs. He went to the
window and looked out; no boy was to be
seen. People were already stirring in the
court below; at least, had the boy's mangled
body been found upon the pavement, the alarm
would ere now have been given. He must
then have escaped through the door, but how?
Truly a difficult question, and one which Feldberg had not now time to solve. Gustavus's
flight filled the false master's mind with mingled fear and rage. The lad had looked too
deeply into his guilty secrets, and must, if possible, be at once recaptured.

In wild haste, he ran down stairs, threw
open the house-door, and hurried through a
multitude of streets and squares in vain; for
nowhere amid the crowd could he discover the
missing boy. Towards midday he returned
home, angry and tired, and heartily cursing
our poor Gustavus.

But who can describe his horror when he found his dwelling in the hands of the police, and himself under arrest? They had searched the premises, and taken possession of his papers and all other suspicious articles. He made several fruitless attempts, to escape the surveillance of the baliffs. His hour had come, and the strong arm of the law was finally upon him. Gnashing his teeth and uttering horrible curses, he, together with the old housekeeper, was forced to follow the policemen, who placed them both in close confinement.

It is not our intention here to follow the course of the ensuing trial; suffice it to say, that, after the lapse of a few days, Gustavus's innocence was fully proved, and he himself released from durance. But numerous complaints from other quarters, supported by unexceptionable testimony, were preferred against Feldberg, and all his cunning, aided by the most unblushing falsehood and perjury, failed to save him. Not only was he proved guilty of fraud and extortion, but also of counterfeiting documents and circulating counterfeit money of his own manufacture. He was sen-

tenced to imprisonment with hard labor for a
long term of years. Thus do the wicked fall
into their own snares! A poor, ignorant boy,
whom with hellish art he had entrapped to aid
him in his reckless schemes, was chosen as the
instrument through which he was to fall under
the strong arm of the law, and society to be
finally delivered from one of the most dangerous enemies to its order and security.

During the same day on which Gustavus
was liberated from captivity, the police officer
to whom he had been first brought sent for
him. The boy's honesty and true-heartedness
had quite won the officer's confidence, and he
felt very desirous to see him settled in some
safe place, where he could learn some useful
occupation.

"My son," said he, "I am glad that you
have got through this ugly business with so
safe a skin. I was really afraid that your four
weeks' tuition under Feldberg might have done
you more harm."

"I was not afraid of that," replied Gustavus,
"for I knew my own innocence."

"You are indeed innocent. Yes, more than

innocent. You are an upright and an honest lad, and you have behaved very sensibly throughout this whole affair. But, how if you had not been able to make your escape? All then might have ended very differently."

"In that case, I should have died."

"What, you would really have had the courage to die rather than commit a crime?"

"Yes! for I promised my father before I left him to be guilty of no wrong. That was the only condition under which he would suffer me to depart."

"Well, it is best as it is. Listen, dear lad; I have something very pleasant to tell you. I know that your purse is not very full."

"Alas!" sighed Gustavus, "I have not a single penny left."

"Fortunately, I can help you. You have rendered a greater service than you yourself are perhaps aware of. Your information has given us the clew to a number of criminal mysteries which had long baffled our penetration. Among the rest, the discovery of the counterfeiter of our treasury notes is no slight service to the state. Some time ago, a reward was promised to the discoverer, and you have earned it."

So saying, the police officer took a roll of money from his pocket and offered it to Gustavus. But the boy hesitated, drew back, and blushed scarlet.

"Well, take it, my child! Only think, it contains fifty good dollars."

"Fifty dollars! And are they all indeed mine?"

Gustavus had never before even dreamed of such wealth. All his blood rushed to his heart. He stretched forth his hand, but it was again quickly withdrawn.

"Ah, sir," cried the boy, "tell me only whether in this affair I have done my duty, — what I ought to have done?"

"Certainly, you have done your duty, — all that you ought to have done."

"Well, then, I cannot take the money!" cried Gustavus, now almost weeping.

"But, why not?" asked the officer, greatly astonished.

"Our master told us that when we had done our duty, only what we were bound to do, we should never take pay for it."

"By heaven! you are indeed a strange boy! Among all the lads in our city, surely not more than one in a thousand could be found as conscientious as you are!"

Thus saying, the officer, in the kindliest manner, laid his hand upon the boy's head and continued: "My child, I honor your conscientiousness. Most certainly, one should not receive payment for a mere fulfilment of duty. But could you not take the fifty dollars as a gift?"

Gustavus's eyes brightened.

"As a gift from your king? The king loves to have upright people in his dominions. You will not be too proud to receive a gift from him?"

"O no! it is allowable to receive gifts!"

Gustavus took the money, and his whole countenance shone as with a new-found delight.

"What will you do with your money?" asked the police officer.

The boy was silent. He was evidently weighing some important purpose; he blushed, and finally asked in low and rapid tones,

whether he could not with his fifty dollars become a painter?

The officer laughed heartily.

" Still at your old notions! Tell me, then,
do you really desire to become a painter?"

" Yes, I desire it with all my heart!"

" This is wonderful! I thought your bitter
experiences would have rendered your residence in the city so disagreeable that you
would lose no time in returning to your country home."

" That would indeed be very pleasant, for it
is much prettier at home than here. But —"

" But what?"

" I cannot return without having accomplished anything."

" And do you think that you will now be
able to accomplish something?"

" Now that I have money. I will be more
prudent, too, in future."

The officer smiled. He walked up and
down the room several times, and then, turning to Gustavus, said, —

" My son, I have an idea! You can indeed
remain here and become a painter —— "

" Indeed !   Truly ? " cried Gustavus.

" Yes, a house-painter."

" A house-painter ! " repeated Gustavus, his sudden delight evidently checked.

" Look round this room !   Observe the blue walls and the gracefully ornamented ceiling. Are they not pretty ? "

" Yes, very pretty ; but — "

" Well, don't they please you ? "

" They are not pictures ! "

" Is that it ?   You have then a notion to be a painter who paints fine pictures upon canvas, — faces, landscapes, scenes, and groups from life.   Come, is it not so ? "

" Yes, I would like to be a painter like Raphael ! "

" Verily !   Indeed ! " laughed the police officer.   " Your aim is certainly lofty enough ! Who put that idea into your head ? "

" No one.   But I am always thinking how much I should like to be an artist ; and almost every night I dream I am a *real* painter, and paint beautiful pictures."

The police officer was deeply interested in the boy's welfare, and sincerely desirous of

serving him. He could no longer doubt that
Gustavus had a decided vocation to the profession of a painter, especially as in searching the
treasured portfolio, he had been favorably im-
pressed with the boy's first attempts. But he
could see no means of overcoming the many
difficulties lying in the way of attaining so
lofty an aim. Hence, speaking very earnestly,
he addressed the lad as follows: —

"My child, what I am about to say is for
your own good. I will give you good advice,
and I think you had better follow it. As yet,
you cannot become an artist. You have not
the means, and your fifty dollars will go but a
very little way. You are also still too young
to battle your own way through the world.
I seriously think you will be forced to begin
with house-painting. I will procure you a
good, honest master, with whom you cannot
fail to learn. If you are diligent, you must in
time earn something for yourself. Meanwhile,
you will become older and wiser. If, after the
lapse of several years, you still retain the desire of devoting yourself to painting as an art,
you will be free to choose for yourself, and the

intermediate time will have been by no means
lost. Come, now, what do you say to that?"

"You think, then," said Gustavus, "that
from a house-painter I could in time become
a real painter?"

"I certainly think so."

"O, then I consent, most joyfully!"

Thus ended an interview which was to exercise a weighty influence upon the future of our
Gustavus. The police officer kept his word;
he found a good master, and a few days later
Gustavus began his duties as an apprentice.

We need scarcely mention that Gustavus
employed his first leisure hours in writing a
long letter to his father, in which all his adventures were duly recounted.

CHAPTER VII.

GUSTAVUS LIVES AND LEARNS AMONG KIND PEOPLE.

THE family which the police officer had induced to receive Gustavus was as respectable as it was charming. The painter, Huber, a man of forty years of age, was upright and honest, full of love to God and man, and beloved by all his friends and neighbors. His skill as a decorative painter was such that he was much prized and sought after, and consequently in excellent circumstances. His wife was not less distinguished for the kindness and gentleness of her disposition, and her household was governed with that quiet industry and tender consideration, which can so well pursue the good and the useful, without neglecting the beautiful and the agreeable.

Three children, the eldest of whom was about twelve years old, completed the happiness of this excellent couple ; for not only were the little ones healthy and well grown, but well brought up ; not only bright and gay, but modest, obedient, and industrious.

A heartfelt spirit of love and peace united these good people into so happy and delightful a whole, that both God and man must have rejoiced over the harmonious concord.

The arrival of Gustavus was of course quite an event for the little family. Master Huber had a large number of journeymen and apprentices, but they all lived out of the house. The kind and considerate police officer had, however, begged an exception to the rule in favor of Gustavus. He had so heartily recommended the boy, and his history was one calculated to excite so much interest, that the family were all in anxious expectation of his arrival. Toward evening he made his appearance ; his manners were modest, but devoid of fear ; and though still preserving all the simplicity of his country breeding, he was neither awkward nor boorish. He was greeted with a hearty welcome, and soon felt quite at home.

"My son," said Huber, "may thy coming among us be blessed to us all! Mayest thou bring peace to our roof, and mayest thou in return receive peace and happiness from us. Poor child! fortune has used thee somewhat roughly, and thy young soul has been fearfully tried! Thou must rest thyself awhile until thou feelest quite restored to thyself. And now, mother, give the lad something to eat."

But the mother had already prepared everything. She kindly invited Gustavus to partake of the little meal she had arranged for him, and the boy needed no pressing. The three children, meanwhile, could not satiate their childish curiosity, but gazed unceasingly upon the stranger. They favored him with sundry friendly nods, and seemed delighted when he held out his hand to them, playfully caressed them, and finally took the baby daughter into his arms.

How different was this reception from that which had greeted him at Feldberg's. He had there been at once repelled by something cold, strange, and fearful, and after the lapse of a few days, had felt as if in some desolate waste, surrounded only by all kinds of reptiles and creeping horrors.

Here, as we have said, he soon felt at home. Every word fell soothingly upon his heart, and every expression bore the stamp of goodness and love. The peaceful atmosphere surrounding the whole household seemed to him like a genial breath from his beloved home. The family soon felt as if they had long known the new-comer, and Gustavus reciprocated all their feelings of confidence and affection. The good always comprehend the good, and where God is, there is always a heart which can find him without fear, doubt, or mistrust. When Gustavus that evening said his evening prayer, how fervent were his thanks for the blessed haven into which he had been safely guided after so stormy a voyage among the rocks and shoals of human life.

The following day, Gustavus made his first attempt in his new profession. There were, in a newly built house, quite a number of rooms and halls to be painted. Huber was delighted at the aptitude displayed by the boy from the very beginning; what then was his astonish-

ment, when in a short time he perceived indica-
tions of talent, a quickness of comprehension,
and a diligence far surpassing his expecta-
tions. The master needed only once to signify
his wishes, to give one example, and the order
was immediately executed as neatly and ele-
gantly as if he had long been acquainted with
all the mysteries of house-painting.

"That is a noble lad!" said Huber one
evening to his wife. "It is a real pleasure to
see him work. He gives his master no
trouble! I foresee the time when he will
tower above me, head and shoulders. He
already does many things better than I ever
attempted, or cared to do them!"

"And he is likewise a good and a pious
child!" added the mistress. "Always willing,
cheerful, and good-natured! I do not think
there is a single grain of falsehood in his
whole composition. It makes him so happy
when he can lend me any assistance. And
how lovely he is with the children! He plays
with them as if he were himself a little child,
and they hang on him like so many burs!"

We will not attempt to describe in detail the

life led by Gustavus in the good painter's
house. Its course was very uniform, divided
between hours of diligent labor and intervals
of repose amid the quiet family circle. The
favorable opinion expressed by Huber concerning his pupil was fully justified. The master
was especially charmed by the boy's extraordinary inventive powers, enabling him to trace
upon paper new and tasteful designs, which he
afterwards transferred to walls and ceilings.
It is true that he frequently deviated from the
prevailing fashion, but every one was forced
to confess that such deviations were justified
by the grace and beauty of his designs. Occasionally, when permitted a larger liberty, and
he could introduce a human face, a landscape,
or a few flowers into the composition, he
worked with all his heart, and it was wonderful how fresh, accurate, and pleasing were the
results of his efforts, and with what magic they
seemed spontaneously to spring from beneath
his busy pencil. By the end of the first year,
the master could safely intrust him with the
most difficult and artistic commissions ; and it
often happened that persons ordering work

would pressingly insist upon having it executed by the lively, industrious, and skilful
boy.

But all this could by no means induce Gustavus to lose sight of his higher calling. The
mere mechanical business of wall-painting
failed to satisfy his soul. The more readily
everything could be accomplished, the less was
he content. He desired to create freely from
his own inspirations, to copy the human face
and the human form, to penetrate the secret
mysteries of nature, and through the magic of
color, bring them to the light of day. This
interior impulse drove him to all the picture-
galleries in the capital, and an art exhibition
which that year took place offered him unutterable enjoyment and delight. What he saw
and thoughtfully considered was stored up in
his faithful memory as a rich treasure for
future use. During his leisure hours, he drew
and painted in his little room to his heart's
desire.

He had set for himself a charming task. He
determined to copy in a larger size the portrait in his locket, — his mother, as he always

called it. She stood so clearly and distinctly before his imagination that he had no difficulty in delineating the beloved features. But often as they were painted and repainted, they failed to satisfy him. In fact, no one could mistake the likeness, but the expression of love and goodness, the heavenly clearness of the eye, and the indescribably lovely smile playing about the mouth seemed beyond his reach. His mother's face had become his ideal of all that was lofty and noble in humanity; no wonder, then, that every copy fell far below his desires and intentions! Those were his happiest hours! For while he painted, his imagination was excited with pondering over the mystery of his birth. Who were his parents? How had he happened to be upon the battle-field at Leipsic? These questions received from his fancy the most various replies, and the most romantic and wonderful pictures were ever floating before his interior vision.

Huber also gave the boy all the aid he could in his higher efforts. He was not properly an artist, but he had considerable knowledge of painting. When he saw how anxious his pupil

was to learn, he imparted to him many valuable pieces of information; he taught him how
to prepare his colors, instructed him in the
laws of perspective, the nature of light and
shade, and gave him many useful hints on the
theory and practise of art. He also lent him
several works upon painting, which Gustavus
frequently studied until late in the night.

Thus did two years swiftly pass away. On
the second anniversary of the day on which
Gustavus first entered Huber's house, the latter
made a little festival. The weather was very
fine, and the whole family went to a neighboring country place. There were found some
graceful acacias in full bloom, and all were
soon seated in the cool and fragrant shade.
The mother had prepared a variety of tempting
refreshments, and the father had brought a
flask of excellent wine.

All were joyously happy, and vied with the
feathered songsters singing amid the branches
overhead in loudly celebrating their delight
and greeting the arrival of another spring.

Suddenly the father enjoined silence, and
said: " My son Gustavus,—for thou art my son

through the love I bear thee, as well as through the affection thou hast ever shown to me,—thou hast now been two years in our house. These have been for us all two blissful years, and I rejoice to say that thou hast added much to our happiness. With thee, a good spirit entered our dwelling to bless us. Thou wert confided to me on condition that I would to the best of my ability instruct thee in my art. I have done so. But thou hast done far more for thyself than I could do for thee. Heaven has endowed thee with such unusual abilities that thou hast scarcely need to learn; thou only requirest once to see and to understand, and thou art quite ready to execute. Thou hast learned more in two years than other apprentices in four; I can no longer regard thee as my pupil. Through thy extraordinary gifts, thou hast done much to widen my circle of business and to increase my reputation. I should be both unreasonable and ungrateful were I not to admit thee to a participation in my profit. From henceforth thou art free. Thou art no longer my apprentice, but my partner and assistant, and thou shalt receive the same remuneration as my other assistants."

Who can describe the speechless astonishment with which Gustavus listened to these words! It was not joy at the announcement that his apprenticeship was over, nor pride in the praise thus bestowed upon him, that so enraptured him; no, it was the true and heartfelt love speaking through every word and penetrating his soul like the mild and balmy breath of spring. He fell weeping upon his master's neck, and cried: "O, this is too much! Far, far more than I can ever have deserved!"

But at that moment the mother produced a basket containing a variety of over and under garments, which with many friendly words she offered to Gustavus in token of her affection. Then came the children: the eldest had woven a crown of spring-flowers which she caressingly placed upon the boy's head, while the two little ones took bodily possession of his hands and knees, embracing him as their elder brother. His heart was so full, so overflowing with emotion, that it was some time before he could recover his self-control and power of speech.

It was quite late before the happy party returned to their dwelling in the city.

Again another year passed swiftly like the last in peaceful uniformity of life. The relations of our Gustavus with this amiable and affectionate family continued unchanged. He never relaxed a moment in that diligence which he regarded as one of the most important aids to the great end he still held in view. His bodily strength and stature rapidly increased; he was soon no longer a boy, but a youth whom one might readily suppose a year older than he really was. His noble countenance, beaming eye, luxuriantly curling hair, and slender but well-proportioned figure, rendered him a universal favorite, especially as, in addition to these physical advantages, his bearing and manners had been polished and refined by his association with the painter's excellent family, without having in the least lost their original frankness and true-heartedness.

Would not any one have thought that amid such fortunate circumstances he must have felt quite happy and contented? But this was not the case. The older he grew, the more he became convinced that he was not in his true vocation. Let him adorn walls and ceilings ever

11

so gracefully and artistically, this could never be anything but a mere mechanical occupation, satisfying neither his mind nor his heart.

Art, to which he was no longer a stranger, had chosen him as one of her favored disciples, and the longing to devote his whole life to her service increased almost to feverish impatience. His thoughts were continually turned toward Dresden, then renowned among the cities of Germany for its treasures of painting, and its appreciation for art. He felt that he would there find all that filled his thoughts by day and his dreams by night.

But could he leave the kind, good people to whom he was so closely knit in bonds of love? His feelings taught him that he had become necessary to them, and that they would suffer much were he now to leave them. What a debt of gratitude did he not owe them? When he stood alone and forsaken in a world of strangers, they had taken him by the hand, and had never ceased to pour around him all the blessings of a father's and a mother's love. Would it not be the blackest ingratitude in him to leave them, now that he had become useful to them, and could in some degree repay them for all they had done for him? No sin was more abhorrent to his kind and tender heart than that of ingratitude.

Such thoughts tormented him unceasingly. He became melancholy and silent, often withdrawing from the family circle, and seeking in solitude counsel and refuge in his perplexities. A hundred times was he on the point of announcing his resolution to his master, and as often did his courage fail before a single glance of that kind and loving eye.

Father Huber and his wife often questioned him with regard to the cause of his sadness, but he ever returned evasive answers, or, to relieve the anxiety of his kind protectors, would vainly endeavor to seem more cheerful.

Finally, one evening when the family were as usual all sitting confidentially together, Huber could no longer refrain from endeavoring seriously to probe the mystery. Gustavus was more silent than ever, and an unshed tear seemed trembling on his lids.

"Gustavus," said Huber, "I must indeed in

serious earnest beg thee to tell me what lies so
heavily upon thy heart, for that thou hast anything upon thy conscience I cannot believe.
Thou canst no longer elude me; I must and
will know the truth."

The youth looked up. His eyes were swim-
ming in tears.

"See, thou weepest," continued Huber.
"That is something quite new for thee, for I
never knew a livelier lad than thou once wert.
It must be something very dreadful to cause
thine eyes thus to overflow."

"Ah! my good master, I cannot tell it!"

"What! Canst thou really have a secret
which should make thee blush to speak?"

"No, oh no, it is not that! I have done
nothing wrong! But ——"

"Come, my son, this will not do. If I am
to aid thee, thou must first of all have confidence in me."

"You insist upon knowing it, and it must
at length be told! I intend, — I must leave
you!"

These words excited the greatest astonishment in the minds of Huber and his wife.

"What! thou wilt leave us? No, we did not expect this!"

"No, indeed, you did not expect this from me! You thought that you had brought your Gustavus up so well, and that he felt so happy with you all, that he would never, never think of leaving you."

"Thou expressest my very thought, and so much the more curious am I to know the cause of this strange resolution."

"You wish to know the cause? You already know why I left my father's house. I did so that I might become a painter. It was then a childish impulse, — no, it was more. It was a voice speaking from within, which, even then, when I scarcely understood its meaning, decided the whole future of my life. I am now three years older, and the voice still calls me; yea, more distinctly than ever. Master, I can no longer withstand it, I must follow where it leads."

Huber was silent a few moments ere he replied.

"My dear Gustavus, what thou hast said troubles me exceedingly. We might have

lived so delightfully together. We regarded
thee almost as our own son, and we hoped thy
affection for us would ever lead thee to dwell in
our midst. I had such fine projects in view for
thee, because I thought thou wouldst in time
learn to love my occupation. But all that is
over; of course, I cannot keep thee if thou
wishest to depart. It makes me very sad; yea,
it pains me deeply."

Gustavus sprang to his feet.

"O, it is just that," cried he, "which
causes me such unspeakable sorrow! I cannot bear that you should think me so wicked
and ungrateful as I must appear to you. What
would I have been if you had not taken pity
on me? Probably a poor, lost creature, or perhaps a mere day-laborer! I must thank you
for all I am and all I can do. And now I
must leave you. Yes, indeed, that is very
ungrateful!" ·

"Well, but who forces you to do so?"

"I have already told you, master. An in-
ternal impulse forces me onward toward the
lofty goal which, since my earliest childhood,
has ever stood before me in the most brilliant

and alluring hues. Art calls me, and I must follow. All my thoughts and all my wishes centre in that one point."

" I am sorry thou thinkest so meanly of my art, that it cannot afford thee the least satisfaction."

" O no, no ; I do not think meanly of it ! How could I do so, when you, my dear master, are so sincerely devoted to it. It is indeed well to adorn the dwellings of men with beautiful colors and graceful ornaments. But is it not still more noble to adorn them with pictures representing nature and humanity in their most elevated and ideal forms ? "

" Thou speakest very boldly, my son ! An artist, such as thou fanciest, must have talent. Art thou, then, so sure that thou possessest this heavenly gift ? In my opinion, it is better to be a good wall-painter, than a mediocre picture-painter."

" I agree with you ; that is indeed the main point. If I have no talent, then am I the most unfortunate man under the sun. But no, I am sure, I *feel* that I have the power to accomplish something excellent. O, do not think me vain because I speak thus. My power is not from myself; it comes from God, and no one could thank God for such a gift more humbly than I do."

"Well, we will grant that! Thou hast talent, thou wilt be an artist. But thou little dreamest of all that is connected therewith. Thou art young, thou seest the world before thee crowned with roses; but the thorns thou dost not see, those sharp, piercing thorns which so often penetrate so deeply and so painfully the heart of the truest artist. Thou knowest nothing of his mental miseries, of his painful renunciations; nothing of the enmity of his rivals, or the fickle favor or indifference of the multitude. He who lovingly embraces the whole world, and bears it transfigured in his heart of hearts, must often find himself mis-known, calumniated, and deeply wounded. The life of most artists is a series of isolated raptures, severe struggles, long sorrows, and bitter disappointments."

Huber spoke these words with great warmth, and then for a time continued thoughtfully silent. Gustavus was deeply moved; he leaned his head upon his hand, and seemed lost in reverie.

"Look at me," resumed the master. "I am no artist; my art is but a somewhat elevated handicraft. I have never had such dreams as seem to torment thee; I have always clung to the golden mean! What then? Am I not happy? Do not my friends love me? Have I not peace and joy in my home? Does not my labor yield me a full support, and have I not always something over to strew the pathway of our more serious life with many flowers? What more can a man desire than to be satisfied with little, and to remain true to his modest calling? This happiness has been secured to thee. But the path that thou wouldest tread leads over unknown wastes to a giddy height. Consider well thy first step, and remember the fate of Icarus. He would fly up to the sun, but his wings melted, and he fell into the unfathomable abyss."

During these words, Gustavus had risen from his seat, and in great agitation walked up and down the room.

"O, you are quite right," cried he. "I

cannot say no to anything you have advanced!
I wish I could! And yet — ”

“ Well, and yet ? ”

“ Yes, you are happy in your vocation, because you are satisfied. But I never could be
happy, because I never could feel satisfied.”

“ Gustavus! Gustavus!” cried Huber, “ these
words from thy lips pain me deeply.”

“ They must be spoken ! My heart demands
something more, something higher! Call me
foolish, capricious, visionary, if you will! I
will grant you everything. But one thing I
must beg, that you do not misconstrue my
heart. I cannot tell you how it pains me that
I must thus distress you. But God knows I
cannot do otherwise. My goal is indeed afar
off; but still it gleams clearly and distinctly
within my soul. What I shall meet upon the
way, joy or pain, I know not. But if I can
only reach my aim, I will cheerfully bear all
that may happen. Master,” — at these words
he seized Huber’s hand and bent his knee before him, — “ Master, suffer me to depart, and
bless me upon my way ! ”

Mrs. Huber had hitherto been a silent but

sympathizing listener. Now that Gustavus
thus imploringly knelt before her husband
(who still hesitated with words of warning
upon his lips), she could no longer refrain, and
said, —

"Father, do not grieve our Gustavus any
longer. Thou seest he is resolved. And
though it pains me deeply to lose him, yet I
believe he is right. I have long observed
something peculiar and unusual in his nature,
which was certainly created to fulfil some lofty
end. The divinity within him impels him onward and upward. His heart speaks too
plainly to suffer us to be deceived. We must
not then deprive him of his happiness and good
fortune!"

"Thanks, a thousand thanks for these kind
words!" cried Gustavus, bending over the
mother's hand and covering it with fervent
kisses.

"But, mother," said the master, "dost thou
not see that Gustavus is indispensable to me?
Who now will invent the newest designs for
me? Who will paint the more splendid and
tasteful apartments? If my business has of

late increased to double its former value, who
must I thank but the lad who always knew
how to find the newest and the best devices?
When he goes, he takes with him my right
hand. But it is not that which troubles me.
It is the boy himself that I shall miss. I have
become so accustomed to work with him, to talk
with him, to love him, that I cannot see what
I am to do without him. It is indeed only my
love for him that makes me so anxious to keep
him with us."

While he was thus speaking, Gustavus had
suddenly left the room, and now returned with
a roll of papers.

"Here! here!" cried he, with a beaming
countenance, as he placed the roll in his master's hand.

"What is this?" asked the latter, unfolding
a number of sheets.

"Pardon, pardon! I have long harbored
the treacherous thought that I would one day
ask for my dismissal; and I fancied I might
perhaps leave something behind me which
would in a measure supply my place."

"Excellent! Beautiful!" cried Huber, as

he examined leaf after leaf with the eye of a connoisseur. On every page were drawings and sketches of wall decorations, executed with the greatest taste and neatness.

"And thou hast drawn all these for me? Drawn them in the night? Eh! thou rogue, thou wantedst to bribe me! Now, indeed, I have stuff enough to work on for two years! And so new and original! A thousand pities that the boy wont be a wall-painter! He would be an honor to the profession!"

Then turning to Gustavus and seizing his hand, he said in tender and affectionate tones: "Thou hast given me great pleasure. Thy designs are very beautiful, and will be of the greatest assistance to me. They do honor, not only to thy taste and invention, but also to thy heart. I now see that I must let thee go; I cannot do otherwise. Go then, in God's name, wherever thy spirit may lead thee. And if thou shouldst ever become a great painter, do not forget thine old master, who is indeed nothing but a wall-painter, but who will not be so envious that he cannot heartily rejoice over the good fortune and the fame of his pupil."

Gustavus fell upon Huber's neck, and thanked him over and over again for this kind consent to his desire. Then, taking the mother's hand, he cried, " And now I have something else for you ; I pray you, come with me, all of you ! "

The whole family, old and young, followed him to his little room. There stood an easel on which rested a covered picture. After hastily placing father, mother, and children together in one group, he drew aside the veil from the canvas; and lo! there stood the whole family, admirably grouped, and well painted! There sat Huber, with his honest, friendly countenance ; by his side, leaning upon his shoulder, was his wife, smiling softly, with her youngest in her lap playing with a flower ; while the eldest daughter stood at the father's knee, and the boy, busied with a book, sat at the mother's feet. A little behind, stood Gustavus, with a beaming face, looking over his master's shoulder. The likenesses were so perfect, that all seemed as if gazing into a mirror. A cry of delight arose, and it was long before the tumult of joy subsided. The happiest of all was Gustavus.

" Thus," he cried, " thus, ye good and dear
ones, thus do ye live in my heart ; thus will
ye ever live therein ! Ah ! I so longed to do
something that might show you my gratitude.
Take, then, this only gift that I can offer you.
The best thing in it, is the love with which it
was painted ! "

" And didst thou really paint that ? " finally
asked Huber, slowly recovering from his surprise.

" Yes, my good master ! That is the mystery which has so long occupied me, and which
has sometimes rendered you uneasy. You
often wondered what I could be doing with
locked doors."

" Listen, Gustavus ; thy picture is excellent.
In the keen seizure of character and the really
artistic grouping, one quite forgets that it is
the work of a scholar. And when I remember
that thou art only sixteen, and that thou hast
had so little instruction, I must indeed wonder
at thy talent. I now say to thee, — thou must
away ! I could not answer to my own conscience were I to detain thee from a path in
which thou mayest become very distinguished."

"And dost thou know," said the mother,
"what pleases me best in thy picture?—that
thou hast not forgotten to include thyself in it.
Thy heart has truly taught thee that thou art
ours, and that thou wilt ever be ours."

"O, how happy I feel!" cried Gustavus.
"May I then, when I am far away, may I call
myself yours, may I believe that you will ever
lovingly think of your faithful Gustavus?
That is far more than I had ventured to
hope!"

The picture was then borne in triumph to
the lower room, and it seemed as if the whole
family could never weary of gazing upon and
examining it.

Gustavus's journey to Dresden was now a
settled fact, and the next few days were passed
in making the necessary preparations. Mrs.
Huber carefully provided all that the most tender mother could deem needful, and the master
secreted quite a considerable sum in one corner of the little trunk.

The parting took place in the light of the early
morning. Gustavus received, with many tears,
the assurances of unalterable affection and the

heartfelt blessing of the worthy pair. His love
and gratitude could find no words. The children were still asleep, and he tenderly kissed
them as they lay in their little beds. When
they awoke, they refused to be consoled, because their good Gustavus had gone away, and
could no longer talk and play with them.

12*

CHAPTER VIII.

A FEW days later, Gustavus reached Dresden. How different was his first appearance in that city from his entrance three years before into Breslau. The then insignificant peasant-boy had become a tall youth, whose dress and bearing attracted the favorable notice of many a passer-by. At the former period, quite inexperienced and unskilled in the ways of the world; he had now grown familiar with its forms and usages, its requirements and its perils, and there was no longer any danger that he would fall a prey to bad men, or become a sacrifice to misleading and bewildering circumstance. He was not, as then, anxious with regard to his daily bread, but through his own savings and his master's generosity, he was the possessor of a considerable sum, quite sufficient, with economy, to keep him a long time above the fear of want. But above all, his end and aim now stood clearly defined before him, and the conviction that he would there find all he had so long been seeking filled him with such cheerful assurance, that his glance was serene, his step firm, and his heart hopeful and courageous.

Gustavus employed the first few days in looking about the beautiful city. Whoever has been in Dresden knows how grand and spacious are its squares, how clean and bright its streets, how tasteful its palaces, and how beautiful its churches! Above all, the Elbe, whose broad stream divides the city into two parts, presents, with its lovely shores, an unrivalled picture. Blooming gardens, fine vineyards, and ornamental country-seats extend to the very horizon, bounded by the waving lines of a mountain range. Gustavus was charmed with the grandeur and beauty in the works both of God and of man concentrated in that lovely spot. But even all these faded into the background the first time he entered

the picture-gallery, one of the finest and most
select in Europe.

There he saw the masterpieces of the most
cultivated nations. Their number and exceeding beauty at first utterly bewildered him,
and his admiration and amazement knew no
bounds. Like one in a dream, he wandered
up and down the great hall, feeling, as his
eye fell upon certain pictures, as if he could
shout for joy, or bow in veneration, until at
length he stood before the celebrated Madonna
of Raphael (the Sistine), the most precious
jewel of the whole collection. When he beheld the glorious queen of heaven, with her
Divine son in her arms, floating above the
earth, surrounded by a glory of angels, tears
of rapture sprang to his eyes, — tears which
not only honored the immortal genius of the
great master, but also gave assurance that the
youth's devotion to art was indeed of heavenly
origin. From thenceforth he visited the gallery
every day.

Huber had named to Gustavus several
painters with whom he might seek to be admitted as a pupil. One of them — we will

call him Roland — was especially celebrated.
Gustavus saw one of his pictures in the gallery, and felt indescribably attracted toward
its author. The painting represented a beautiful mountain landscape, with aged oaks and
pines, bold rocks and rushing streams, — the
sun was just gilding with his first rays the
mountain-tops, and the clouds floating in the
transparent blue of heaven; in the foreground,
beside a little hut, knelt a hermit lost in devotion, and praying to the great Creator of the
glorious nature around him. All lay in solemn peace and silent beauty, announcing the
greatness and goodness of Him who, with almighty power and infinite love, rules over
the works of his creation.

Gustavus often returned to this picture, and
soon had an opportunity of seeing the painter
himself, who, accompanied by several ladies
and gentlemen, stood before his latest production. His noble figure and benign countenance made a deep impression upon our young
friend, and filled him with a burning desire
to be guided by him through the higher walks
of art. But how could he approach him, how

in his lowliness hope to be regarded and
hearkened to ?   He gazed long and intently
upon the master's face, and when he left the
hall followed with a heavy heart, not venturing to approach or address the object of his
veneration.   Thus passed several days.   When
Gustavus was alone, he felt quite self-assured,
imagined the most delightful interviews, and
fancied his desire almost fulfilled.   But as
soon as he directed his steps toward the
painter's dwelling, or accidently met him in
the gallery or the walks, his courage failed,
and he felt too shy to intrude himself upon
the man with whom he had linked all his
hopes for the future.   Finally, however,
chance, or rather that higher Power, which,
unknown to us, so often guides our destiny
into new pathways, came to his assistance.

One fine morning, Gustavus went to walk
amid the lofty and beautiful trees in the
" Great Park."   The luxuriance of nature
blooming round him, the freshness of the fra--
grant air, the clear sunlight gleaming in a
thousand sparkles through the quivering leaves,
the warbling of the birds intoning their joyous

hymns in the depths of the groves, all rendered him inexpressibly happy. The future
lay hopeful and smiling before him ; if Master
Roland were there, he would surely have courage to present his petition. When lo ! as he
stepped forward toward a shady nook, his
eye fell upon a gentleman sitting on a bench
alone. He was not mistaken, — it was the
master. He was certainly occupied with some
grand and beautiful conception, for he was
gazing thoughtfully before him, and drawing
figures on the sand with the end of his cane.

A slight tremor ran through Gustavus's
every limb, his blood rushed tumultuously
toward his heart. He was about turning
modestly away ; but no, thought he, now or
never ! I shall not have such another opportunity. He stepped softly forward, and, lifting his hat, stood near the end of the bench.
He hoped the master would observe and address him. In fact, the slight rustling near
him had roused the painter from his reverie.
He turned a long and searching look upon the
youth, who, with downcast eyes and modest
mien, stood before him. Finally, he asked in

a serious, but by no means a harsh tone of voice,—

"Do you wish anything from me?"

"Yes," was the almost inaudible reply.

"If I do not mistake, I have often seen you before in the picture-gallery. You seem to place yourself in my vicinity."

"I desired to attract your observation. Now I am fortunate enough to venture to speak with you."

"Sit down, then. The morning is fine. We will talk a little. And, first, who are you?"

"My name is Gustavus Braun. I am a painter, or, rather, I desire to become one."

"Aha! now I see. You are poor; do you wish assistance?"

"No, no," cried Gustavus. "I have not much, but all that is necessary. My wishes go much higher."

"Indeed! then I can scarcely aid you."

"O yes! You can,—you alone!"

"You excite my curiosity. What is it?"

"Suffer me to kiss your hand?" said Gustavus, fairly overcome by his feelings.

"This is extraordinary!" cried Roland, drawing back the hand which the youth had seized and kissed.

"I have seen a picture of yours. O, so beautiful! I have no words to express it!"

"And is this all you have to say to me?"

"O no! Much more. But I am afraid!"

"Well, then, I suppose I am not to hear."

"My desire is so great, that, were it not fulfilled, I should be very unhappy."

"So much the more do I wish to know it. No one shall be unhappy if I can prevent it."

"You wish to know it? Well, then, I would like to be your pupil."

These words were so softly spoken, that Roland was obliged to ask a repetition. He was greatly astonished. Doubting whether he had heard aright, he looked up to the youth, who was gazing upon him with suffused and imploring eyes.

"This is indeed quite unexpected. No pupil until now has ever thus introduced himself. I almost think I shall be unable to grant your request."

"O, that was what I feared!" cried Gus-

13

tavus, his eyes filling with tears. "It would have been too much happiness. How could I think that so renowned and great a man would condescend to look down upon me, a poor and unknown youth!"

"Young man, judge for yourself. You are entirely unknown to me. I am ignorant of your parentage and circumstances; I knew nothing of your previous education or of your capabilities. How then can I, without further information, receive you as my pupil?"

"May I, then, tell you the simple history of my life?"

"I beg you will do so."

Gustavus told all; his life at home, his journey to Breslau, his adventures with Feldberg and Huber. His manner, at first hesitating and timid, became as he proceeded lively and enthusiastic. He especially dwelt upon the fact, that since his earliest childhood he had been impelled by some powerful inward pressure toward the art of painting, and that his every desire centred in the hope of becoming one of her most devoted disciples.

"Thus, then," said he, in conclusion, "came

I here. I felt that here, if anywhere, the goal might be attained. All that I have seen since my arrival in this city, the grand and the beautiful, have only stimulated my desires into a quenchless longing. And must I stand by the living spring, and not be suffered to satisfy my thirst? Must I see the golden apples of art hanging before my eyes, without venturing to stretch forth my arm to pluck them? O, kind sir, have pity upon me! Only be my master, and I will be the most docile and obedient of your pupils!"

Roland had listened with amazement and ever increasing sympathy to this passionate discourse. This was evidently no ordinary youth. His eyes flashed, and his cheeks glowed. The painter thought he had never seen finer features, or a more noble expression of countenance.

"My dear young friend," said he, "I see that you have at least a passionate love for art. But that is not enough."

"O, I know, I know! You mean talent?"

"The word Art is derived from roots signifying power, capacity. To be able is the main thing. What is it you can do?"

" I fear I can as yet do very little."

" But the capacity to do, the ability, must
exist. I have made it a rule never to encour-
age mediocre talent. I owe this to my art.
There are bunglers and daubers enough in this
world ; I shall certainly do nothing to increase
their number."

" Then you think if I had talent, real talent — "

Gustavus left his sentence unfinished. A
ray of hopeful joy beamed through his soul.

" Then, indeed, we might consider the matter. My friend, art is difficult, the aim is
lofty, and the way long and arduous. There
are few, very few, who know the goal, and
have courage and strength sufficient to climb
the steep and narrow path."

" O, I know the goal ! "

" Tell it me then ! "

" Raphael's Madonna ! " cried Gustavus.

A sudden blush colored his cheek, and a
smile played round the painter's beautiful,
earnest mouth.

" Indeed," cried he, " that is very bold !
And do you hope to become a Raphael ? "

"Alas! I know that is impossible! God has thus endowed but one man only; but are not the truly great and noble sent upon the earth to charm the eyes and inspire the hearts of lesser men?"

"You are right! One must indeed strive for the highest if one would pass the common bounds and rise above mediocrity. But the way, my friend, — have you forgotten that the way is long and steep?"

"Have you not just said that it was the part of courage to climb?"

"Truly, of steadfast, enduring, and self-sacrificing courage."

"I pray God daily to maintain and increase it in me!"

"Then you think you already possess it? Well, it shall be put to the proof! Only you must not think that to study painting is to wander in a garden of roses. The mere painting is but of secondary consideration; practice alone can effect but little. You must study; you must comprehend the human soul as well as the human body; nature must be open to you, not only in her external phenomena, but

13*

also in her hidden spirit; the history of humanity and of the arts must lie before you as an open book. I might say that there was no sphere of solid or elevated learning which the true artist should not embrace in the spirit of love."

" O, I had divined all this," cried Gustavus, " and now it stands wonderfully clear before my soul. For that very reason, my dear sir, do I require a master, to learn all aright, and properly to embrace the whole with my understanding."

" And now enough, my dear friend. I must thank you for a very pleasant hour. We will hereafter speak of the rest. Come to me this afternoon, and we will see what can be done. Do you know where I live ? "

" O yes," cried Gustavus, with difficulty repressing his delight. " I have often stood for hours together before your dwelling, without daring to enter."

" Wonderful youth ! " thought Roland, as he walked away. " Can it be my good fortune to have had a diamond thrown in my way, which, when polished, will emit the most glorious light ? "

Intoxicated with delight, Gustavus followed the master. He thought he had finally reached the long-desired aim. He felt inwardly convinced that if he were permitted to lay before Roland some specimen of his capabilities, he would not be rejected. The hours of the forenoon crept slowly on, and, long before the appointed time, he stood before the painter's house. Three o'clock finally came; Gustavus entered with a beating heart, and was directed by a servant to Roland's studio, with the information that he was there to await the master's arrival.

He gazed curiously around. The studio was a large, cheerful, and tastefully furnished hall, commanding a view into a beautiful garden. A number of young persons were variously employed; some ground and prepared colors; others were drawing from casts; others, again, were painting at their easels; on the walls hung several fine pictures in handsome frames. Gustavus's entrance for a moment interrupted the busy but noiseless labors of the students, but all eyes were soon again turned upon their several employments. After the lapse

of a few moments the master entered, and his
friendly glance fell at once upon the youth who
stood in a respectful attitude near the door.

"Ah! thou here?" cried Roland. "Thou
hast not let thyself be waited for; a proof that
thou hast happily overcome thy fear of me."

This address sounded so kind and hearty,
that it banished every remaining feeling of
timid anxiety from the young man's breast.
He also regarded it as a good omen, that the
master in speaking to him, instead of you, employed the more familiar thou.

"I already feel quite sure thou hast a real
love and appreciation for art. But I would also
like to know what degree of skill thou hast
actually acquired. Wouldst thou be willing
to give me some little specimen of what thou
canst do?"

"That is my most anxious desire!" replied
Gustavus.

"Canst thou draw from thine own head?
I mean, canst thou design a little group without having any pattern?"

"If the exercise be not too difficult, I will
try."

Roland thought a moment.

" Come," said he, " sketch the scene of our meeting in the great park this morning. Only a rapid sketch ! Nothing finished ! "

Gustavus trembled with delight. Aided by his excellent memory and his lively imagination, he had always been most successful in his portraiture of human countenances. He cast a long and steady glance upon Roland's face, and then moved onward to the designated place, where he found paper and the necessary drawing materials. He chose the moment when he found Roland sitting on the bench, lost in thought, and when, with imploring mien he first approached him. The master, meanwhile, went to his easel, standing near a window, where, with a steady hand he worked upon a large painting.

After the lapse of a half-hour, Gustavus cried out, —

" I am ready now ! "

" Let us see then ! I am really quite curious to know how thou hast succeeded ! "

So saying, Roland took the paper, and scarcely had it met his view, when his countenance assumed an expression of the greatest astonishment.

"Great Heaven!" he cried, "this is well, very well done! What excellent likenesses! What firmness! And how beautifully the whole is managed! This is far more than I expected!"

Gustavus's delight at these words was so great, that bright tears rolled down over his cheeks. At that moment the door opened, and an old gentleman of dignified exterior, but friendly countenance, entered. It was Count Sommerfeld, who thought he could not better employ his large property than by encouraging true art and assisting worthy artists. He was very intimate with Roland, and often visited his studio to enjoy the beautiful pictures, and the master's intellectual conversation.

"Come here, Count!" cried Roland, "here is something really extraordinary. Do you see that youth, still half a boy! He accosted me, while I was taking my morning walk, with the request that I would be his master. Of course I thought that very strange, and probed him severely. But he stood the trial bravely. I bade him come to me this afternoon, and have just given him a subject to try his powers. Look, the picture speaks for itself!"

The Count gazed sympathizingly upon the little group, and then said: "And what will you do, my good friend? The petition set forth by this picture seems to me so eloquently expressed that you cannot well refuse it."

"Indeed! What will I do? If I do not take him, he will go straight to some other master, and I shall lose the pleasure of for once cultivating a real talent!"

"Agreed, then!" said the Count. "You must keep the youth, whose face besides pleases me greatly. But you must also leave me a share in your good work. I will prove him further, and see what I can do for him."

This short conversation was held in the recess of a window, at a little distance from where Gustavus stood. When it was concluded, Roland approached the youth and said, —

"Thy desire shall be fulfilled; I have decided to receive thee as my pupil. Thou must find thee a room in my neighborhood, and come to me every morning at seven o'clock. Of the rest, we will speak hereafter."

Gustavus had no words to express his gratitude and joy; he could only seize the master's hand and fervently press it to his lips. He then hastened to his own dwelling. His first impulse there was to fall upon his knees and thank God for all the happiness he had sent him; his second, to draw forth his beloved locket, and in silent communion with his mother's image, confide to her all that had happened. When he became more quiet, he poured forth his joy in two letters which were severally despatched to his foster-father, Braun, and his recent master, Huber.

In fact, no life could be better or happier for our Gustavus than that which he led under the guidance of the painter Roland. The latter was an artist in the fullest sense of the word, quiet, sensible, and full of deep and creative enthusiasm for his art. His instructions, especially the conversations into which he frequently entered with his pupils, were in the highest degree useful and inspiring, and made, upon Gustavus, who eagerly caught every word, the deepest impression. It seemed to him as if a veil had suddenly been withdrawn from many mysteries which he had half divined, but whose causes and principles he had been unable to discover. The best understanding also subsisted between Gustavus and his fellow-students; as they all united in love and veneration toward their master, they were all good friends, and the young man, for the first time in his life, enjoyed the pleasure of association with persons of his own age, engaged in similar pursuits.

It was especially fortunate for him that he had won the regard of Count Sommerfeld. When that nobleman visited the studio, he frequently conversed with Gustavus, questioned him with regard to his past life, and criticised his efforts. He also permitted him the use of his fine picture-gallery and excellent library. The old man soon observed that the youth was lacking in general cultivation, in the knowledge of many branches of learning indispensable to his career as an artist. One day he said to him, —

" Gustavus, dost thou know what, after virtue, chiefly adorns every man, especially every artist ? "

" I think, modesty ! " replied the youth.

14

"That, too! But that is not what I mean. I am thinking of something thou dost not as yet possess."

Gustavus looked up inquiringly into the old man's face.

"Thou hast told me thou hast never been at any except a village school."

"Alas! it is indeed so."

"The consequence of which is, that thou art quite ignorant."

"I wish I could deny it."

"Thou must no longer remain so. Dost thou desire to become a real, a genuine artist?"

"Yes, that is my most earnest desire."

"Thou knowest well that more is required than a happy talent and a skilful hand. These are both necessary to produce excellence, but they will not alone suffice to create works which shall elevate as well as delight the contemporary world, and hereafter stand as landmarks far above the levelling stream of time. A spirit, my son, is needful, which, nourished by every noble science, shall be able with certainty to decide upon the true, the good, and the beautiful. Now, canst thou not tell me what most adorns an artist?"

"Ah yes!" sighed Gustavus, "knowledge! And that I have not."

"Thou art right! Knowledge! A knowledge which shall on every side cultivate the mind and the heart. I do not mean that it is necessary for the artist to be a professed man of science, but he must be sufficiently familiar with the whole range of human learning to be able to draw forth the gold and the silver for his own art. Thinkest thou, thou couldst be a reasonable landscape painter without an accurate knowledge of nature? Couldst thou succeed in a historical picture without a true insight into the spirit of past ages?"

"Then I can never be a true artist!" said Gustavus, with a heavy heart.

"Thou must make up all that is lacking to thee."

"I would cheerfully do so! But you forget, Count, that I am poor."

"I will take care of that. I will procure thee masters, and Roland will spare thee the necessary time. The chief and the best part

depends upon thyself alone ; namely, the interest, desire, and industry with which thou wilt
devote thyself to serious study."

And thus it was. The good Count procured
for Gustavus the best masters, and the youth
devoted each day several hours to the study of
history, natural science, and modern languages.
An eager desire to learn, and great quickness
of mind, gave him great advantages, and he
made rapid progress in every branch.

CHAPTER IX.

WHO ARE MY PARENTS?

THUS, amid the most fortunate and agreeable circumstances, did our Gustavus pass two happy years. If we have succeeded in conveying any just idea of the young man's extraordinary capacities and genuine love for art, our readers will not be surprised to learn, that under the guidance of so eminent a master as Roland, aided by the spiritual encouragement and assistance of the excellent Count, and surrounded by all the treasures of art, and the ever-living intellectual activity of the art-loving city, he had become a distinguished artist. Having taken the prize at an exhibition of the Academy of the Fine Arts, his pictures being remarkable not only for their admirable execution, but also for their spirited conception and deep significance,

14 *

his name was already pronounced with respect. In addition to this, the elegance and beauty of his youthful figure, the noble simplicity of his manners, and his finely cultivated intellect, gained him the love of many, as well as an entrance into the higher ranks of society.

Roland, at the end of two years, had declared that Gustavus could no longer be his pupil; he must now pursue the paths of art supported by his own powers, and relying upon his own genius. The young man found the needful pecuniary support, partially in a small pension from the government, procured for him by the Count, and partially through the sale of his paintings, which were much prized and sought after. He already began to dream of a journey through the cradle of the arts, the dream-land of every artist, beautiful and soul-entrancing Italy.

The older Gustavus grew, the more frequently and earnestly did the question force itself upon him: Who am I? The mystery enshrouding his birth, which he had long, by a thousand suppositions striven to penetrate, hung above his life like a dark cloud, and ever

allured the working of his restless imagination,
continually adding new fancies to the old.
Were his parents still living? Who, and
where were they? How could he win an answer to this important question? He could
find no clew to the labyrinth. His secret was
to him so sacred and holy that he had hitherto
silently concealed it in his own bosom, and
had confided it to no one, not even to his dear
Count.

To ease a little his restlessly beating heart,
he determined to select the wild battle-scene
with which, when a little child, his fate had
been entangled, as the subject of a large picture. His lively imagination was busied in
bringing together all that it had presented to
him as possible, or probable. His reasoning
was nearly as follows: A baby, such as I then
was, could scarcely have been found in such a
fearful scene, unless its mother had been
near. But what could have induced her, a
delicate woman, to place herself and her child
amid the dangers of a battle-field? She certainly must have been the wife of a French
officer, and her love for him must have im-

pelled her to follow him at a short distance
from the army. She probably deemed the
unfortunate issue of the battle impossible, and
thus found herself overwhelmed by the confusion of the flight. In the tumult, her carriage
was overturned and thrown into a ditch, whence
she was deprived of all means of proceeding
further. But how had she been separated
from her child ? Must not one surely think
she would have died with him rather than
forsake him ? This fact seemed explicable
only by the supposition of the presence of some
more powerful affection. The place where the
carriage was found had evidently been the
scene of a fierce struggle between the flying
and their pursuers. And might not his
mother's husband, his father, have been
among the former ? She became aware of his
presence, saw him wounded before her very
eyes ; in the agony of mortal anguish she
rushed toward him, forgetting the child which
lay in the bottom of the carriage.

Here, however, ended all his suppositions.
How his mother had quitted the battle-field.
why she had not returned for her child, and

what had been her subsequent history, were facts lost in the impenetrable darkness of the mysterious past.

From the above data, Gustavus designed his picture. The conception was bold, and in the broadest style. A horrible confusion of French and Prussian troops; on the faces of the combatants on either side, heroic determination and despairing rage, or overwhelming courage and the joy of victory; scattered between, rearing horses, broken cannon, wounded and dying men; in the foreground, a French officer of lofty and noble stature sinking wounded from his battle-steed, while a young and beautiful woman, — wonderfully like the picture in the locket, — rushing forward, with love and horror in her face, seizes him in her arms, — were the most prominent objects in the composition. A little to one side was the broken carriage, and in it the child, whose peaceful slumber and angelic innocence presented an indescribable contrast to the fearful scene surrounding it. Over all floated the misty atmosphere, the melancholy gray of a late autumn evening.

The picture was finished. Gustavus had painted it with all the strength of love and sorrow within his soul. He was almost sure that it represented a portion of his own history, and thence was it especially dear to him. He also thought it nearer to the high ideal he had ever before him than any of his previous works. He had long wished to present some faint token of his gratitude to the good Count, to whose fatherly affection he was indebted for so large a portion of his present happiness. What if he were to beg him to receive the picture as a gift? A suitable opportunity was near at hand; in a few days the Count would celebrate his birthday. He could at the same time confide to him the mysterious circumstances of his own childhood, for he had determined no longer to conceal them from so kind a friend. The thought of seeing his favorite picture in the hands of his beloved benefactor filled him with such delight, that he looked forward with longing expectation to the arrival of the happy day.

The birthday came. Gustavus had the picture taken to the Count's palace, and hung in one of the lower rooms. He then went up to the Count's chamber, where he met with the usual cordial reception, and where, in a few heartfelt words, he offered his congratulations and wishes for future happiness.

"Thou wishest me happiness," said the old man. "But thou forgettest that I am to-day seventy years old. What the world calls happiness no longer exists for so aged a man. *We* live alone in the past and in the future. Memory and hope fill our being. Happy is he whose memories are peaceful and whose hopes are joyful. We must at every moment be prepared to lay-down the staff at that shadowy bourne dividing this world from the next."

"No, no," cried Gustavus, deeply moved. "The sun of your life will long shine in the heaven whence it has so mildly and blessedly beamed upon my days."

"We will leave that to a higher power; let us now speak of thee. It is one of the greatest pleasures of age to find itself renewed in the blooming youth of others, and to watch a development so like, and yet in many things so unlike its own. The mysterious dispensations

of Providence have, alas! deprived me of the
pleasure of thus following the growth of my own
sons and grandsons. So much the more happy
am I to have found in thee a consolation for my
declining days. I have regarded thy progress
with the greatest delight. Thy life has indeed
been as the flight of the young eagle toward
the sun, and I rejoice that it has been in my
power somewhat to strengthen thy wings."

" And I would willingly show my gratitude.
But how can I, when I have nothing but my
good-will, and all I could possibly do would
still fall so far behind your kindness? And
yet I have made a slight attempt. I have finished a small work, and it would give me great
pleasure if you would receive it in token of my
boundless love and gratitude."

" What! A picture? I like that! I will
receive it with pleasure. Where is it?"

" In one of the lower rooms. May I ask you
to go down with me?"

At that moment a side door opened, and a
noble looking lady entered. Although no
longer young, — for she was apparently about
forty, — she still bore the traces of great beauty.

Her countenance was lovely but pale, and a close observer could not fail to perceive traces of sorrow and suffering left upon it by severe struggles and trials. Her eyes possessed uncommon gentleness and tenderness, and their expression became still more beautiful as they turned upon the old man a smiling glance of inexpressible affection.

ı "Ah! thou art just in time!" cried the Count. "Dear Gustavus, that is my daughter, the widowed Baroness von Adlersberg. Even the long distance from her estates to Dresden could not prevent her coming to surprise me with her good wishes on my birthday. My dear daughter, this is the young painter, Gustavus Braun, of whom I have already spoken to you."

The lady kindly offered the young man her hand. "My father has told me much good of you, and I am the more rejoiced to have met you."

Thus saying, her eyes rested long and searchingly upon the youth's countenance, and some dark cloud seemed to dim her beautiful eyes.

"Well, you will soon learn to know each

15

other better!" said the Count. "And now let us go. Gustavus has prepared a surprise for me. A picture awaits us that we must see at once."

They went. Gustavus felt strangely moved. He knew that the Count had a daughter who led a lonely and retired life upon her own estates, but he had heard nothing of her arrival, which had only taken place the evening before. He found it impossible to account for the singular sensations which the sight of her had awakened within him. They reached the hall, and stood before the picture which had been hung in an excellent light, but was still covered with a heavy curtain. With a trembling hand the young man tore away the veil, and the battle-scene stood before them in all its fearful truth.

But how utterly indescribable was the impression it made upon the beholders. The Count seemed totally bewildered, and the Baroness stared with a look of unutterable horror upon the picture. She became deathly pale. Her eyes seemed starting from their sockets, her limbs trembled, and her form bent breathlessly forward.

"For God's sake," cried she at length, "what does that picture mean?"

"It represents a scene at the last battle of Leipsic," replied Gustavus.

"Leipsic!" repeated the Baroness, in faint tones. The shock was too great. Her strength failed and her consciousness fled. Her father and Gustavus were obliged to support and lead her to a seat.

"In the name of Eternal Love!" cried the Count. "Gustavus, explain! explain!"

"What I have here represented I learned from my father," replied Gustavus, trembling, and pale as death.

"How! From thy father? I do not understand—"

"My father was a Prussian soldier in the battle of Leipsic."

"But the child! the child!" cried the Baroness, who had now recovered from her momentary faintness.

"The child was carried from the battle-field by my father."

Like a sudden flash, these words penetrated the Baroness's every nerve. She rose, seized

the youth's shoulders with both her hands, and
in heart-breaking tones cried out : —

"And it lives? it lives?—no, do not answer! It would kill me were you to say no! —
Great God! you make no reply ; — does the
child then live ? "

"It lives," replied Gustavus, who now could
with difficulty master the storm of feeling within his own bosom.

The Baroness sank upon her father's breast.
"It lives! it lives!" she repeated softly, but
with almost superhuman joy. "But where?
where ? " cried she, again turning to the youth.
"Where is my son ? "

"Here, at your feet!" exclaimed Gustavus,
embracing, with unutterable rapture, the knees
of his finally found mother.

No; joy does not kill. Else would the Baroness surely have fallen a victim to the violence
of her emotions. But God who had just shown
his marvellous providence and his wondrous
guidance of events, gave her strength to resist
their overwhelming power. She sank on her
knees before Gustavus, flung her arms around
him, buried her face in his curls, and gave vent

to her feelings in unrestrained sobs and tears.
The old man stood near, laid his hands caressingly upon the heads of his daughter and
his grandson, and lifting his eyes to heaven
said : " My God ! On this day hast thou blest
me unutterably ! "

The Baroness had no strength to rise. Gustavus joyfully took her in his arms and gently
laid her upon a sofa. He knelt near, and
drawing the locket from his bosom, opened it
and said : " Do you know this picture ? "

" Great God ! " she cried, " that is the locket
I hung upon thy neck the very day on which
thou wert first deprived of thy mother's care."

" Yes, that is the dear jewel which has again
united me to my beloved mother. O my mother, for how much must I not thank this picture !
It has been the talisman which has protected
me in peril, encouraged me in every struggle,
and incited me to press ever onward toward a
higher goal. God told me it was my mother.
I never doubted it for one moment. O, I knew
you long before this meeting ! You may now
understand how I came to represent you so ac-
curately in my picture."

"Yes, I see; while still unknown to each other, the power of love has mysteriously watched over and between us. I also am conscious of no moment in which I have not thought of thee, but in fact, chiefly that I might become accustomed to seek thee only among the angels in heaven. Ah, my son, the tears I have shed for thee and thy dear father are more than could be counted!"

"And my father?" asked Gustavus, with a slight tremor in his voice.

"O, that he were among us to enjoy this day! But he is looking down upon us from the habitations of peace. He is no more. The day on which I lost thee, cost him his life.

The Baroness wept. Gustavus sought to console her, and fervently covered her hand with the most tender kisses.

"My children," said the Count, "not now these sad remembrances; the joy of the present is so great that we would be ungrateful were we only to think how we could still increase our happiness. We are all too deeply moved. Without, in the fresh air, under the green trees, we will feel more composed. Gus-

tavus shall there relate to us all the occurren-
ces, great and small, of his eventful life. You
will thence see, my beloved daughter, that thou
hast not only found a son, but a worthy, ener-
getic, upright, and noble son!"

They went into the garden, the mother leaning on Gustavus's arm. There, by turns walking in the shadow of the lofty chestnuts, or
sitting on the garden seats, they suffered their
most cherished memories to flow forth in the
full stream of love and heartfelt confidence.
Gustavus related the story of his life, and the
warmth with which he spoke of his benefactors,
the honest Braun, the upright Huber, and the
noble Roland, showed that happiness had only
elevated and ennobled the best feelings of his
soul. We may imagine how attentively the
mother listened. With the utmost tenderness
she hung upon his every word, now interrupt-
ing him with loving questions, now caressingly
stroking his handsome head, then kissing him
with her soul upon her lips, and then again
shedding tears of fervent gratitude and joy.
Could one imagine a higher delight for a mother, than thus to see unfolded before her eyes

the blooming and hopeful life of a son whom she had long wept as dead, and who was now restored to her loving arms?

The news of the wonderful event which had taken ·place in the Count's palace ran like lightning through the whole city. The intimate friends of the family came to learn the truth, and to offer their congratulations. Gustavus, now Baron von Adlersberg, and heir to a large property, was the hero of the day. Many had previously admired his genius; to this was now added the lustre of a distinguished name and great wealth.

Among the rest came Roland. The Count had previously sent him a sum of a thousand dollars to be divided among such young artists as he should think most deserving. The painter came to thank him. He was received with open arms. After heartily embracing Gustavus, he took him aside, and said, —

"How is it? Will you now turn your back on that art which you have to thank for a great barony and a happy home?"

"No, indeed!" replied the young man. "That would be the blackest ingratitude!

On the contrary, I will henceforth be only so much the more her grateful and devoted worshipper."

"That is right," said Roland, "that is just what I expected. Believe me, art is *still worth more* than a title and a full purse!"

"I know that!" cried Gustavus. They cordially pressed each other's hands. They had mutually understood each other's souls.

In the evening, when the happy trio again found themselves alone together, Gustavus said: "Now, dear mother, grant my prayer, and tell me all the circumstances that have caused our lives to be so sadly and strangely sundered."

"Alas, my son, it is a melancholy history! But thou art right; thou shalt hear all. We shall feel freer and easier when we have once looked the dark past steadily in the face."

The Baroness leaned back a few moments on her sofa, as if to recover her self-possession; Gustavus sat on a stool at her feet, and a little apart the old man had fallen asleep in his arm-chair.

"It was," began the Baroness, "during the

year 1811 that I first learned to know thy
father, the Baron von Adlersberg. He had
been sent to our court in Dresden by the King
of Westphalia. His handsome person, noble
heart, and cultivated mind attracted me toward him. Our love was mutual, and, with
my father's consent, I became his wife."

"Do you know, dear mother, that I am delighted to learn that my father was a native
of the country in which I have had my own
growth and education. I should feel really
sorry to be forced to regard any other land
as my fatherland, or to bear a foreign name.
My foster-father and I both thought I must
be the son of a French officer."

"No, my son, thy father was a German;
but like many of his countrymen, he rever-
enced the rising star of the great Emperor
whose powerful genius at that time swayed
the destinies of Europe. He had already accompanied Napoleon through several victorious campaigns, and had risen to the rank of
a colonel. His knowledge and ability had
rendered his offices necessary in the adjust-
ment of the kingdom of Westphalia, and he

had been temporarily withdrawn from active
service. During that time I became his wife;
we lived at Cassel; one happy year quickly
passed; thy birth filled us both with unspeakable joy; we were so lost in our own happiness, that we did not see the clouds gathering
upon our horizon. The destruction of the
great French army in Russia soon followed;
Germany and half the world again lifted their
heads and reasserted their independence.
There was an immediate and extraordinary
call to arms; my husband, among the rest,
was forced to resume the sword. We parted;
I, with a bleeding and ill-divining heart, remained behind. The struggle raged on, the
fiercest struggle known to modern times. At
first came news of victory; by degrees the
bulletins became less and less hopeful. The
French army was driven nearer and nearer
to Saxony; my husband's letters ceased to
reach me. I was in despair. Had he been
wounded? Was he dead? I knew not; I
could not fly to him to watch over him if
living; or if dead, to weep beside his grave.
Finally a letter came; only a few lines, an-

nouncing that the French army had concentrated near Leipsic, and that a decisive battle
was expected. My heart beat with joy; he
was still alive. But at the same time a feverish longing arose in my soul to see him, or at
least to be near him. Thou seest it was mad-
ness for a weak woman to leave the peaceful
circle of her home and venture out amid the
tumultuous waves of that wild storm of nations. But love does not consider, — will listen to no reason; it only follows the blind in-
stincts of the heart. One morning I ordered
my carriage and entered it with thee, for it
would have been impossible for me to leave
thee behind. I came to Halle, and there we
heard the distant, stifled roll of the heavy ar-
tillery. Two days passed in death-like sus-
pense and agony. The most contradictory
rumors met our ears; now it was the French
who were victorious, and then the Allied armies. I could no longer endure the tortures
of uncertainty. I determined to be at least
nearer to that spot where every bullet might
perhaps be aimed at my husband's heart.
On the unfortunate 18th of October, I left

Halle, and slowly, but as if drawn by some
unseen power, proceeded on my way to Leipsic.
The coachman wished to return, but I refused,
and commanded him onward. A false report,
received from some French soldiers galloping
past us, that the Emperor was triumphant, increased my self-delusion. I approached within
about a mile and a half of Leipsic, but there
— to my horror — I met the first columns of
the flying French army. In frantic haste they
stormed past us. The confusion became every
moment greater. The road was blocked up
with cannon and baggage-wagons; I could
neither advance nor recede. My carriage was
thrust aside, and sank with its hind wheels in
a ditch. The horses attached to a cannon fell;
mine were at once unharnessed and seized upon. Innumerable bands of men fled by me,
but no one thought of me; one sole idea filled
every mind, — to press onward as rapidly as
possible. But the horror was doomed still
further to increase. The position seemed a
favorable one for some columns of the Guard
to station themselves, and cover the rear of
the flying army. Gustavus! I soon found

myself in a raging combat. A regiment of
cavalry rode rapidly past; the bullets whistled
round my defenceless head. My eye suddenly
fell upon one detachment of the cavalry; a
single horseman led them on. It was he,—
my husband! As if stricken by lightning, I
sprang up; my eyes stared after him, my arms
were outspread toward him. But he did not
see me; with a loud and menacing voice he
gave his orders. Holy Father in heaven!
Suddenly he fell; a ball had struck him.
Like an arrow I sprang from the carriage.
How I reached him through the tumult of
battle and the close ranks of the combatants,
is still a mystery to me. I can remember
nothing, except that, with a cry of horror, I
fell upon him, and flung my arms about his
neck; all consciousness then left me."

Overpowered by these fearful memories, the
Baroness could no longer continue. She
buried her face in the sofa-cushions, and gave
free vent to her emotions. Gustavus had
listened with breathless attention, and at this
moment cried out: "Wonderful! wonderful! All this has often passed in darkened
images before my inward vision."

When the mother had somewhat recovered her self-control, she lifted her head, and said: "Yes, tell me, my son, how was it possible for thee to represent that fearful scene in thy picture, so nearly as it really occurred?"

"It may have been an inspiration from above to reunite us," replied Gustavus. "And then could it have been otherwise? Could I, a feeble child, be found upon a battle-field unless my mother had brought me there? And what could have severed her from my side, if not the power of some stronger affection rendering her insensible to danger, and excluding everything except itself? How probable the thought that it could only be the sight of her husband's peril which could tear the mother from her child. Among all the possibilities which passed through my mind, this seemed to me the most true to nature and the dearest. Thus, from a chain of probable suppositions and plausible conclusions, arose my picture. It was God's will that I should have divined aright. But continue, dearest mother; I burn with desire to know all that followed."

"I have but little more to add," replied the
Baroness. "Thy father was severely wounded.
But his faithful followers, who were fervently
devoted to him, were not willing that he should
die on the battle-field, or fall into the hands
of the enemy. They laid him, as well as myself, for I was still unconscious, upon a bag-
gage-wagon, and, soon after, the retreat was
slowly and in good order continued. I finally
recovered my senses. My first thought was
my child! My heart-rending cries moved even
the rough soldiers lying wounded with me
upon the wagon. I would have sprung out;
they held me back. It would have been easier
to have swam against a rushing mountain tor-
rent, than through that dense retreat to have
reached the place where I had left thee. Thy
father's hot and feverish grasp held my hands
fast bound in his; his dim and dying eyes were
fixed upon my face, and a faint smile upon
his lips betrayed that he had recognized me.
Gustavus, I saw him die before my eyes. I
cannot understand why I did not then die
too, but God willed that I should still live on
and suffer. After a few days we reached

Erfurth. My husband's faithful body-servant had assumed the care and protection of his master's wife. I there fell into a nervous fever. During several weeks I lay a prey to the wildest delirium. I recovered; but it was three months before I was strong enough to leave my room. My first journey was toward the place where a frightful destiny seemed to have deprived me of every joy in life. I could scarcely recognize the place; it was covered with a thick and melancholy veil of snow. Ah, what efforts I made! How many thousand means did I employ to discover thee! All in vain! Finally, I buried thee in my heart with my beloved dead. I withdrew in the deepest solitude to one of my husband's estates, and there, through a long night of sorrow, wept over my brief dream of happiness.

"And henceforth?" cried Gustavus, tenderly folding his arms around his mother's neck.

"Henceforth I will be more cheerful! I will again live my life in thee!"

Mother and son remained long locked in a silent embrace. Then awoke the old man, who

gazed upon them with a look of unutterable
love, and finally said: "Do you know, my
children, what is now our first duty? Gratitude!"

"Yes, O yes!" joyfully cried Gustavus.

"We must now thank those kind people to
whom we owe far more than we can ever
repay."

"You mean, Father Braun and good Master
Huber!"

"Exactly so. I think you had both better
go and visit them."

"Delightful! charming!" cried Gustavus.
"And you, dear mother, will you not accompany me?"

"Canst thou doubt it? Must I not tell them
they have made me the happiest mother in the
world?"

The next day but one was fixed for the departure of mother and son upon their journey.

CHAPTER X.

ALL'S WELL THAT ENDS WELL.

WE again find Gustavus in Breslau, whither he was accompanied by his mother. Of course he visited the worthy pastor and the excellent police officer, who, after his flight from Feldberg's, had shown him such real kindness and sympathy. Their reception was hearty, and their joy great, when he imparted to them the sudden and happy turn which his fortunes had taken.

But we must not so hastily pass over his visit to Huber. He purposely chose an evening hour, because he knew that the master would then be at home. He preferred entering the family in which he had passed so many happy days as son and brother, simply as Gustavus. For he justly feared that his new name and position might create some strangeness and embarrassment between himself and these simple people. The announcement of the last important event in his life was intrusted to a letter to be left with them at his departure. It was already dusk when he knocked at the well-known door. The master called out: "Come in!" Gustavus entered, and once more, with the old heart and the old love, stood in the cozy little room among those kind, good people. He joyfully bade them good evening.

"Merciful Heaven!" cried the mistress. "That is Gustavus!"

The master rose quickly from his seat and flung his pipe aside.

"What! Gustavus?" cried he. "Truly, it is he. Welcome, a thousand times welcome, my dear, good boy!"

Embrace now followed embrace. The children came too, and soon joyfully surrounded their unforgotten brother. Only the eldest daughter, now grown up into a pretty maiden of some sixteen years, stood half ashamed at a little distance, and blushed as Gustavus kissed her blooming cheek.

Huber, with all his fluency, seemed as if he could never sufficiently express his joy.

"The thousand!" cried he, "how the lad has grown! When I think of him as he first came to us, — and now he is a full head taller. And how straight and strong he looks! That is a youth after God's own heart. And he looks distinguished too, like a young nobleman!"

There is no telling how long he might have continued in this strain, had not the mother interrupted him, saying: "But father, art thou not going to ask our dear young guest to sit down?"

"Yes, indeed, yes; he must sit down; here, in this comfortable corner. Mother! this is a real festive evening. Bring out the best thou hast. And don't forget a flask of good wine; for this my son — I had nearly said — was lost and has been found again. No, not lost! But returned! The young, aspiring artist, lauded by all the papers, has not forgotten the old and unknown wall-painter, John Huber!"

"O, I never feared that!" said the mother; "I knew Gustavus would never forget us."

"A thousand thanks for your kind opinion.

of me!" cried Gustavus. "I return to you
the same as of old!"

"The same as of old?" exclaimed Huber.
"No, thou every day becomest something new.
Gustavus, what all hast thou not become since
thou left us. I saw thy picture at the late
exhibition. That *was* a picture! When I
looked at it, bright tears ran down my cheeks.
I went there twenty times, only to see what
great eyes the people made. I did so long to
cry out and tell them all that thou hadst once
been my scholar. But nobody would have
believed me."

"Did I not tell thee," said Mrs. Huber,
"that Gustavus had been created for better
things?"

"Yes, indeed! And thou wert right. Thou
art always right!" he added, smiling. "I,
too, knew that he could not remain a mere
wall-painter; but then it grieved me so when
he wanted to leave us!"

"Ye kind, good friends!" cried Gustavus.
"Say no more; ye will spoil me. If I were
proud and arrogant, it would really be your
fault. How is it now," added he, after a

momentary pause, — "how is it with your business, master? I hope it is as good as ever!"

"God be praised, yes! Thy drawings, Gustavus, were a real blessing to me. Wherever I used them, every one was delighted. Every one insisted upon having rooms and halls painted after those patterns."

"Well, they must be nearly exhausted. If you like, you shall have some new ones."

"What, thou couldst? .... But no! Thy talent is much too lofty, thy time too precious —"

"Say no more," interrupted Gustavus. "Would it, then, be something so very extraordinary once more to return to one's old occupation, especially when one receives such excellent testimonials of ability? Besides, I have now abundance of time."

"How so?"

"I am going to look a little about me in the world."

"What, hast thou no fixed residence?"

"Not for the present. I am now in Breslau, visiting my old friends. In a few days I am going among the mountains to see my dear Father Braun."

" And then ? "

" Then, master, I hope to realize an old and heavenly, lovely dream. I expect to visit Italy."

" Gustavus, Gustavus, the muses must have been very kind to thee."

" Yes, every earthly blessing has been vouchsafed to my unworthy self."

" Come, tell us, tell us ! "

" Not now ; you shall hereafter know everything ; but all I can tell you now is, that Heaven has blessed me unspeakably."

Thus continued the conversation. Gustavus told of his artist life in Dresden, played with the children, and questioned Mrs. Huber concerning all the little events of a household life. An excellent supper, at which a flask of noble wine was not wanting, increased the general hilarity, and it was late before Gustavus rose to depart. The good mother was quite unwilling he should leave them, as she had already prepared a bed for him in his former little room. But he was not to be persuaded to remain. When parting at the outer door with his old master, Gustavus pressed a letter into the kind hand which clung to his so cordially, and seemed so loath to suffer him to depart.

We will remain behind a few moments with the house-painter's family. The father soon returned to the sitting-room; old and young were still assembled, for the general joy had kept the little ones awake.

" Gustavus has put a letter into my hand," said Huber, " and I must see at once what it means."

He went to the light, opened the paper and read; and the more he read, the more astonishment did his countenance express.

" What is this?" cried he. " Braun not my father, — lost child, — battle of Leipsic, — mother found, — Baron von Adlersberg! Listen mother; listen children!" cried he suddenly. " It is really wonderful! listen to what Gustavus writes! "

Mother and children, all filled with anxious expectation and curiosity, pressed round the father, while he read aloud Gustavus's letter

containing a condensed account of the singular
and fortunate unfolding of his destiny. The
letter concluded thus : —

"Pardon me, dear master, that I have
chosen this mode of informing you of all that
has befallen me. But I wished to appear
among you only as Gustavus, and show you
that the old heart full of love and gratitude
was still beating within my breast. But I
could not entirely withhold from you the
knowledge of this great change in my circumstances, for you have a right to rejoice in all
my joy. Retain for me your old affection, as
mine for you can never fade from my bosom.
Regarding my mother's enclosure, I have only
to add, that you must by no means consider
it in the light of gratitude, but merely as a
proof of her desire to render the future paths
of your children as easy and agreeable as possible."

When Huber opened the sealed enclosure,
a note for three thousand dollars fell out of
it. Within were written simply the following
words : —

"The money is for your children. May

they ever tread in the footsteps of their excellent parents! But for you is the grateful
heart of a happy mother!"

We will leave the good painter's family to
their astonishment, their joy, their heartfelt
expressions of affection toward Gustavus, and
return to the young man, whom a few days
later we find with his mother on the way to
Reichenthal.

As long as this little village had been in existence, never had it witnessed an event similar
to that which took place one fine summer afternoon, in the year 183–. A coach and four
rolled past the lowly huts and cottages, and
the post-horn blew such a blast that all the
mountains echoed. Young and old ran to the
windows or out into the street; the coach
rolled past the church, the parsonage, the
school; ever up the hill, whence all, however,
knew that the only roads leading further were
mere wood-paths.

Finally, the equipage stopped before the
forester's door. Braun's hounds bayed; the
mistress of the house gazed astonished over the
humble railing. A handsome young man

sprang out of the carriage, and running up to her, shook her heartily by the hand.

"God bless you, mother!" cried he, in tender and affectionate tones. She stood as if rooted to the earth, gazing in amazement upon the youth, who seemed to her so strange, and yet so familiar.

"What," cried she, finally, "Gustavus?"

"Yes, I am he."

Her face beamed with delight.

"God be praised that thou,—that you are once more here. How glad I am; and how my good husband will rejoice!"

"Where is the father?"

"In the wood."

Then calling a brisk little lad to her side, she said: "Run, Christy, run for thy father! Thou knowest where he is, down by the last wood that was cut. Tell him to come at once, there are guests here!"

The lad ran as if winged by the winds. Meanwhile, Gustavus's mother had also left the carriage, and cordially greeted the forester's wife, who seemed utterly bewildered with the distinguished air and elegance of this strange apparition. She drew timidly back, and Gustavus, who wished to reassure her, took her aside, and smilingly said to her: " Mother, how is it? Are you satisfied with me now?"

" Ah! Gustavus, of what do you remind me?"

" Not *you*, but *thou*, should you say to me. Else I will think you are not glad to see me, and that you wish me away again."

" Well, if thou wilt have it so! — When I think how often I treated thee badly, how often I scolded thee, and did not love thee as I should have done, then I am so angry with myself. Ah! canst thou forgive me?"

" Mother, say no more of that; and if you indeed love me a little, let me never hear you speak such another word. Think only how you wept when I went away, how you filled my bundle with new, clean clothes! That stands for ever graven on my heart!"

The forester's wife now invited her guests to enter the house; but Gustavus said they would prefer remaining in the open air until

Braun returned. The good woman slipped away, probably to exchange her every-day garments for others more suited to the reception of such distinguished guests.

"Dearest mother," said Gustavus, as he led the way into the garden, "let me show you the favorite places of my childhood! Look, on this barn-door I made my first essays in art. Time and rough weather have washed them all away! But no! There is still the crest of the stately knight whom it gave me such unutterable satisfaction to counterfeit. And there, too, are the donkey's ears and the traveller's hood. Under those wide-spreading pear-trees I have often, for hours together, lain in blissful reverie. I remember well how a finch had once built his nest on one of the lower branches. It was a real delight to watch how the old fed their young, and how gay and sprightly the whole little household seemed to be. That apple-tree I planted myself. Only see, there are seven or eight golden apples shining through the leaves."

They left the garden and entered the wood.

"Ah, mother!" cried Gustavus, "these noble oaks and elms furnished me with the scene of my happiest games and dreams. Here, on this very spot, whence the eye takes in the whole broad valley, I often sat and dreamed, gazing into the far blue distance. The mysterious foreshadowings which then filled my bosom have all since been most strangely and most gloriously fulfilled."

At that moment, Gustavus heard a rustling in the bushes behind him. He turned. Braun stood before him. One spring, and the youth was locked in his arms. "Father!" "Gustavus!" was all these two happy souls could utter. When the first emotion had somewhat subsided, and the long embrace was loosened, Braun's eyes fell inquiringly upon Gustavus's companion. The youth took her hand, and leading her to Braun, said: "Father, look, this is my mother! Dost thou hear, I have found my mother!"

The Baroness seized the forester's hands, pressed them to her heart, and cried: "Thou saviour of my Gustavus! Noble, true, and excellent man! My lips are too feeble to

express the gratitude welling from my happy
heart. God will reward thee!''

Braun uncovered his head, looked piously
heavenward, and said: "My God, thou art
indeed great!"

They then proceeded slowly toward the
house, where they found the good dame
and her children in full state. That was a
happy day in the forester's home. Gustavus
related everything as it had happened, and
Braun was often forced involuntarily to ex-
claim: "Lord, thou hast done all things
well!"

Late in the evening, Gustavus said to
the forester: "And thou must accompany us, father! I cannot again part from
thee!"

"No, thou hadst better leave me here! I
should be entirely out of place in thy noble
society, among thy distinguised relatives. I
am too old to learn new ways. Here, in the
forest, among the hills, is my place, with my
bucks and does. If thou wilt only always love
me, and sometimes let me hear from thee. I
shall be entirely satisfied.''..

" But how, if thou wert to be head-forester ? "

" How so ?   Head-forester ? "

" Yes, to my mother.   She has a forest that
extends over half a square mile ! Oaks and
firs that three men could not span ; deer, stags,
roes, wild boars, and pheasants in such abundance that they would delight thy heart ! And
then a house for the head-forester in the very
centre of the wood ; in the stable, two fine
horses ; and on the meadow, twelve Swiss
cows, with tinkling bells.   Hey ! will not that
content thee, father ? "

Braun's honest heart beat with joy.

" Agreed," cried he.   " I consent.   I am
yours, body and soul !   That will be a life ! "

We must here end our tale.   Gustavus, during the following year, went with his mother
to Italy, where he more and more perfected
himself in his chosen art, to which he was
never, for a single moment, faithless.   His
paintings, glorious testimonials of the beauty
and depth of his soul, were the delight of his
contemporaries, and will bear his name to

future generations with honor and reverence. Braun's family removed to the estates of the Baroness, where, in the most delightful relations with the inhabitants of the chateau, they led a happy and contented life.

FIDDLEHANNS.

FIDDLEHANNS.

One beautiful summer evening, a well-dressed young man entered the public room of the inn known as "The Eagle," in a Silesian market-town. He had just dismounted from his horse, which he had recommended to the special care of the host. With an air of aristocratic indifference, he flung his riding-whip and cap upon the table, and took a rapid survey of the assembled company.

It consisted of the host, of the bailiff of the estate on which the town was situated, of the schoolmaster, and the district judge; consequently, of the chief personages of the market-town. The host stood, cap in hand, before the stranger, and with the most submissive courte-

ry asked the commands of the " gracious lord,"
as he was pleased to term the unknown guest.
He had, at the first glance, convinced himself
of the faultless beauty of the new-comer's horse,
its value had been quickly calculated, and he
had thence deduced the probable weight of the
owner's purse; an all-sufficient reason for the
excessive attention he stood ready to bestow
upon the traveller.

While he was thus engaged, the bailiff, the
schoolmaster, and the judge had drawn a little
closer together, and were exchanging various
remarks upon the stranger, with sundry guesses
as to what had led him from the great high-
ways to their little, unfrequented town.

They listened attentively to every word that
fell from his lips, and when he said to the host:
" A glass of wine, but of the best!" they concluded from his accent that he was no Silesian.

The host brought the wine, and although the
vintage failed to please the stranger, the host
appeared quite indifferent, as the guest said in
a disparaging tone: " The wine is good enough
for this neighborhood ; one must cut one's coat
according to one's cloth. You, gentlemen, are

probably from the village," continued the traveller, turning to the other guests, " or, rather,
I should say, from the city," added he, cor-
recting himself with a smile.

"The market-town, with your lordship's permission," replied the schoolmaster and the
judge, who on being addressed had quickly and
reverentially risen from their seats; the bailiff
followed their example, but somewhat more de-
liberately, that he might yield no portion of
his dignity.

" You can, then, probably tell me something
about my cousin, old Baron Hammerstone; he
must lead a curious sort of a hermit's life in
his old fortress of a castle. Is it indeed true,
that he is now entirely invisible to every one ?"

This was a matter in which the bailiff felt
himself quite at home. Having learned that
a relative of his master's stood before him,
he suddenly became more gracious than before. Shrugging his shoulders and assuming a
thoughtful mien, he replied: "It is indeed a
fact, your lordship. The older the Baron
grows, the less will he know of mankind; yes,
I really think he has taken up a hatred to the
whole world."

"But why so? Has he had any especial cause to do so?" said the stranger.

"No one knows," replied the bailiff. "The Baron is so now, and we cannot change him. It is a great pity he should be possessed by such a crazy whim, — I had almost said, — I meant to say singular fancy. Our gracious lord is so really good, that whenever he can help any one, he does it most willingly, and with both hands full."

"Every one in the town knows that," here interrupted the schoolmaster, who as he proceeded became quite enthusiastic; "you would hardly believe how deeply in debt our community was some thirty years ago, when the Baron bought the Lordship, and — without vanity be it spoken — how many rogues we had among us. I well remember how my blessed predecessor in the school, while I was only his assistant, once had his cow stolen from its stall, and how the next day the thieves' children brought him the poor creature's tail, because his old cowskin was rather the worse for wear; the old man was so indignant that he never recovered the shock, and soon after died. I, too, found it bad enough in the beginning, although we had a brace of rascals in the stocks every week. But now, look at our community! Everything is entirely changed! That we have no more debts, we must thank our gracious lord's kindness and generosity; but we have a still deeper cause for gratitude to him, which is, that our townspeople are now all upright and excellent men. He taught by his own good example, and mild and considerate as he was to all who without any fault of their own had fallen into trouble, just so severe was he toward every rascal. In short, he has the best heart in the world, and it is a thousand pities he should have become so misanthropic."

"I must, however, believe that my excellent cousin was not always thus?" remarked the stranger in an inquiring tone.

"Your lordship is quite right," replied the bailiff.

"At first, it was not quite so bad; still, he had a slight attack of this same indisposition, if we may so call it, at the time when he first purchased this property, and set the old castle in order. During the first few days, he had

new chains put to the drawbridge; since then,
it has always been kept up, and the old lord
remains within his castle as if it were a beleag-
uered stronghold. During the first few years,
all had free access to him, at least every Sunday; he then listened attentively to every com-
plaint, and was ever ready to give money, good
counsel, or consolation. In those days he kept
a cook, a huntsman, and a serving woman.
But since his marriage, they have every one
been discharged."

"How is that?" cried the cousin in surprise.
"I had not heard a word of any marriage.
Since my fifteenth year I have been in the Eng-
lish service, at a great distance from this hermitage,—namely, in the East Indies; and,
besides, I never had the pleasure of meeting
the Baron face to face. From what noble
house, then, has my cousin taken a spouse?"

"She was born Countess Strahling," replied
the bailiff, who now seemed to be in the full
tide of his eloquence.

"Yes, indeed! you are still a young man,
gracious sir, and the Baron is nearly seventy;
of course you would not know him, having been

so long absent. The story of his marriage is a
very strange one. One morning when as usual
I knocked upon the drawbridge, the Baron
himself lowered it, and I entered the lower
court-yard; he was dressed in his handsomest
Sunday suit. It was a real pleasure to look at
him.

"'Resch!' said he to me (that is my name),—
'Resch, go down to the town, order my horses
at once, for I will go out; and tell the pastor
to be in the castle chapel at four o'clock precisely.'—'At your Grace's command!' replied I, turning away to execute my commission. In a few moments the horses were harnessed; the Baron jumped into the carriage
and drove off; the pastor got ready, and at
four o'clock stood with me in the castle chapel.
As the clock struck, the Baron drove back to
the great door; the huntsman sprang down
from his seat and opened the carriage door,
when lo! to our amazement, a lady followed
the gracious lord from his carriage. Who was
it? The young and portionless, but singular-
ly beautiful Miss Strahling, who dwelt in our
neighborhood with some distant relatives of

her father's. The Baron led the gracious lady into the chapel, introduced her to the pastor as his betrothed, showed him the marriage contract, which had been carefully executed in all due form, and requested him to proceed with the marriage ceremony. The pastor hesitated, because the banns had not been published; but the Baron showed him a royal license, and informed him that I, the huntsman, the cook, and the maid, were to serve as witnesses; and thus the marriage was at once concluded."

During this recital, the cousin could not help several times laughing aloud. The bailiff continued: " The wedding was followed by a princely feast, — a real masterpiece of good cooking. The gracious lord sat alone with his bride at one table; the pastor and I occupied a second; and, at a little distance, the maid and the huntsman were seated at a third. Our lively Fiddlehanns, who was not then quite so old as he is now, stood at the door and played the violin to his heart's content; but the newly married pair remained sitting quite still and serious, and consequently the rest of us did not venture to move. At the end of the next hour, just as the clock struck, the Baron laid aside his napkin, rose, offered his lady-wife his arm, and led her into an adjoining apartment, where her bridal gifts were all laid out; there were in gold, silver, jewels, and deeds the full value of $ 80,000, as I, being bailiff of the baronial estates, can testify upon my honor and my conscience. 'That is your property, madam,' said the gracious lord ; ' and, in addition to this, you will receive a yearly income of one thousand dollars, under the sole condition, that, during my lifetime, you will never again enter this castle; you are otherwise free to act as you please; I desire to exercise no control over you; and now I have the honor to wish you good morning.'

"At a sign from the Baron, the huntsman gathered together the costly gifts, and placed them in the carriage, which was still standing with the horses unharnessed in the court-yard. The Baron then gave his wife the customary documents, led her reverentially down stairs, and sent her back a rich lady to the friends from whom he had received her a poor girl."

"Well, and was that really the end of the whole matter?" asked the cousin, laughing.

"I most humbly beg you to wait a moment," replied the bailiff, who, with considerable emotion, added : "I have my own ideas upon the subject. I think the Baron felt toward his wife an unutterably tender affection, but fancied she never could be happy with him. I must indeed be sadly mistaken if such were not the fact, and if he did not intend, in the noblest and tenderest way, by the sacrifice of his own dearest wishes, to render her wealthy and perfectly independent, so that she might use her free choice in seeking out whatever she might deem her surest way to happiness. These are my honest convictions, which, however, I have no right to offer as certainties ; — but I have already gossiped more than there was any occasion for."

"Worthy, estimable old man !" said the cousin, clapping the bailiff on the shoulder; "you were impelled by your excellent heart, and the impulse was an honor to you. But what has become of my cousin's wife? If she, as it appears, really cherished no affection for him, I presume she soon obtained a divorce and married another?"

"Not so," replied the bailiff; "she is still free, and, so far as I know, she honors the Baron as if he were her father; notwithstanding her wealth, she is not happy, because she well knows that the Baron is not so, and she has but one single desire, — to see him once more. She has often tried to induce him to permit her to visit him; but he has hitherto steadfastly refused, and I know him but ill, if the reason of his apparently harsh denial be not, that he fears lest his feelings at such an interview should overpower him. This is indeed the most wonderful of all his wonderful whims, — that he is ashamed of possessing a kind, gentle, and affectionate heart: he takes the greatest pains to seem rough and hard-hearted, so that no one may think him weak. Probably, at some former period of his life, he was deceived, and his confidence abused; probably — But what right have I to make suppositions concerning my lord's

conduct! Enough, he must have been sadly
treated by his fellow-beings, that he should so
entirely avoid them ; and even now, amid all his
loneliness, like an invisible guardian-spirit, he
seems never weary of doing good to all."

"Mine host! Another bottle of wine!"
cried the cousin ; and when the wine was
brought, he poured out full glasses for the
bailiff, the schoolmaster, and the judge, in-
viting them to drink to the health and welfare
of the old lord. No one required a second
invitation, and even the host poured out a
glass from his own private cupboard, and
drank with the rest.

Meantime, the cousin's countenance visibly
darkened ; he walked several times up and
down the room, and finally exclaimed : "This
is indeed too bad ! Here have I come a couple
of thousand miles to see my strange, dear,
good cousin, and to talk with him over some
important family matters ; and from all I hear,
it may be that he will not even permit me
to enter the castle. Very vexatious, — upon
my honor, very vexatious!"

"Without doubt he will deny you admit-tance," replied the bailiff; "I know him well. After his marriage he sent away the cook, the huntsman, and the maid, and has all his food, which he will allow no one but Fiddlehanns to bring him, thrust through a sliding window in the castle gate."

"Fiddlehanns?" said the cousin inquiringly.

"Yes," continued the bailiff, evidently quite excited by the subject of his discourse; "and how it does look up there! When I pay my customary business visit on the first of every month, and look through the open window into his chamber, I feel really desperate. The dust and lumber of many years lie so thick upon the floor, — I assure you I do not exaggerate, — that the path made by the Baron's footsteps as he walks up and down all day long, looks just like a little valley between two ridges."

"Oh, oh!" cried the cousin, "that is too bad!"

"But not worse than the reality," continued the bailiff; "instead of human beings, the Baron has only old musty books and docu-

ments for companions, and I have more than
once heard him remark, with bitter scorn,
that they were just as arrant liars as men
were ; but that what one could not easily accomplish with the human race, he hoped to
effect with books, namely, to make them in
their own despite witnesses to the truth. God
only knows how much paper he has already
written up! And that too is all covered with
dust. I believe he sent away his servants,
not only through hatred of men, but also because he wished to render himself secure from
every attempt at preserving order and cleanli-
ness in his vicinity ; he often forbade old Chris-
tine meddling with his affairs, but she never
would listen to him, and he finally drove her
away — so to say — in anger at her neatness.
But now his secret almoner, Fiddlehanns,
brings her her wages regularly, the first of
every month, just as if she were still in the
Baron's service."

"Who, then, is this Fiddlehanns?" again
asked the cousin, and this time more earnestly than before.

"Our gracious lord's favorite, and our old

humpbacked musician," replied the bailiff;
"the Baron is a great lover of music, which,
after his studies, forms his only recreation in
his solitude. He plays the flute, and Fiddlehanns accompanies him on the violin; he
remains within the castle with the drawbridge up, and Fiddlehanns stands without
on the other side of the moat, and plays as
long as the Baron likes. The latter seems
to love and trust the old musician more than
any other living human being; yes, I believe
he is the only mortal who has the least influence over our gracious lord. If you have
indeed such weighty matters to discuss with
the Baron, your best plan will be to apply
to Fiddlehanns; if he cannot win you an entrance, you must renounce all hope. But see!
here he comes himself, as if he had been called.
Good evening, Fiddlehanns!"

The old humpbacked musician, with his violin under his arm, entered the public room.
One could hardly fancy an uglier man, and
yet it was that very ugliness which had procured him the special affection of the recluse.
Besides, as soon as the old musician began to

speak, his pock-marked features were lighted
up by so benevolent an expression, that one
soon felt kindly toward him, even when one
failed to understand his peculiar mode of
speech, and the meaning of the searching but
furtive glances cast by his great brown eyes
from beneath his heavy gray eyebrows.

Fiddlehanns had, however, not always been
thus. In his childhood he was as comely a
lad as one would wish to see, and there were
still a few aged persons living in his native
village who could remember, when very young,
gathering round the good-natured boy whose
violin was the delight of the little community,
and whose kind heart rendered him a favorite
in every household. A severe fall had checked
his growth and deformed his person, and the
small-pox had disfigured his once attractive
features.

The bailiff soon made Fiddlehanns acquainted with the person, the position, and the
wishes of the stranger, who on his side, by
obliging expressions, strove to render the old
musician propitious to his cause. Fiddlehanns cast his eyes upon the cousin, smiled,

and instead of replying, drank off at one
draught the glass of wine which the schoolmaster had pushed toward him; then placing
the violin under his chin, he played in the
strangest fashion, beginning with a pleasant
dance, then changing to a funeral march, here
and there interspersed with snatches of dance
tunes. Suddenly he broke off with a horrible
discord, and gave the bailiff such a piercing
look, that he cried out: " That air sounds very
familiar to me! Did you not play that dance
at our gracious lord's wedding?"

The old musician passed his hand across
his eyes, replaced his violin under his arm,
and thus addressed the stranger: " The glorious sun must shine, sir cousin, the moon no
less; and the green grass and the whole world
must live! You dear people, vain is death;
but not in vain is music, and not in vain one
single kind word spoken. Yes, look at me,
what a selfish fellow I am! Not so, Mr. Bailiff?
Do you not know me as such? Good! — our
master cousin must also march out and make
a beginning. If you only knew, sir cousin,
how down in the wood lies a poor cottager

on his deathbed, with wife and children, and
never a roof to shelter him. I have just come
from there. The storm that so threateningly
thundered this afternoon fell in fact upon the
poor cottager's thatched roof. How it blazed!
How the wind blew and drove the poor people
from their burning dwelling; and how they
had not far to carry their treasures, and yet
were tired and breathless with the exer-
tion of saving them; namely, the wife, her
sick husband; and the eldest boy, his two
little sisters; — you should have seen that from
afar, as I did! And now the sick man is lying
out under God's free heaven; the rain is
washing the death-damps from his brow, and
the wind is piping the old song in his ear: ' I
have set my heart upon nothing you see!' and
the wife is kneeling beside him, warming his
cold finger-ends in her trembling hands, and
the children are sitting round, the silly things,
and crying for bread, as if it could fall from
the trees like the heavy rain-drops. Up and be
doing, gentlemen! Here is my hat; I have
done playing, and now I must ask my reward."

So saying, Fiddlehanns went hat in hand from guest to guest, and collected a liberal alms, which he placed in the schoolmaster's keeping, at the same time saying: "How is it, godfather? Could you not beg a couple of beds from your old wife? And you, Mr. Bailiff, have you not a couple of shirts to spare? To-day we must for once be before our gracious lord and get the people as fast as possible under shelter, procure bread for the children, and medicine for the sick. When our lord will hear it to-morrow, he will be angry, and that is just what I want, for then I can say to him: 'It serves your Grace just right; that is what one gets by leading such an owl's life!' But now you must all go to the wood! And take the pastor with you, — you may want him; and master cousin, too, — every little helps! If you do well by those poor people, master cousin, I will see what I can do for you with the gracious lord."

Thus saying, he turned to leave the room, but at the threshold, once more faced the stranger, and after a few moments' consider-

ation, cried out: "Sir cousin! Be at the
drawbridge to-morrow at ten o'clock in the
morning! Good night!"

He then hastened up the hill nearest to the
castle, and only separated by a deep ditch from
the tower in which the recluse was accustomed
to sleep. The twilight grew ever fainter,
while the moon in all its splendor rose behind the wooded crags. The old humpbacked
musician gazed a few moments upon the scene,
then tuning his violin, he said: "A farewell
to the sun and a greeting to thee, old friend
moon! Be content; the poor fiddler will do
his best."

Baring his head and standing thus amid the
solemn silence of the landscape, he played the
air of the song: "Now rest all the woods
and fields."

The well-known tower window was then
opened; the old recluse appeared with his
flute, waited until the violinist had played to
the end, and then began to pipe the same air
upon his instrument, which Fiddlehanns accompanied with his violin; the nightingales
amid the shrubbery of the neglected castle

garden soon added their delicious notes to
the nocturnal concert.

The melody had long been ended; the two
strange old men stood silently facing each
other until the twilight had faded into dark
night, and the moon, which had meantime gotten behind the tower, threw its dusky shadow
upon the figure of Fiddlehanns, when the
Baron asked: "Where have you been, Fiddlehanns?"

"Far and near," was the reply, — "in wood
and field, amid men and all kinds of creatures, — among the rest in a certain castle,
which I shall not name. Well, she has at last
solemnized her wedding, — that person whom
I will not name, — this afternoon, at five
o'clock, just after the storm had ceased."

"You lie!" cried the Baron hastily. After
a short pause, he continued in low and suppressed tones, — tones of ill-concealed anguish: "It is all right, I should have said;
I rejoice in her happiness; I have never desired anything but her happiness. Yes, yes,
I thank God that she has finally found the
right one to make her happy." He was again

silent a moment, and then asked: "Who is the bridegroom?"

"*Death!*" replied the old musician. "A glorious rainbow was just spanning the castle towers as I came to the door and found the people running hither and thither; old blind Lena, lame Mathew's children, and widow Margaret with the weak back, beside half a dozen more of their acquaintance, were weeping and praying and condoling together. I asked what was the matter, and just at that moment the maid came down and told them their gracious lady was dead; I ran up the steps, for I felt that unless I saw it with my own eyes, I could not believe that the poor had lost their good angel; and sure enough, there lay the beautiful earthly vesture which the pure spirit had laid aside and left behind. Then I went down into the thickest wood, took my violin and played:

'Commit thou all thy ways,
And all thy heart may wring,
To Him whose love and praise
The distant heavens sing.

To clouds and air and wind
He giveth course and way,
And paths He 'll surely find
Wherein thy feet may stray.'

While playing, I thought of all those who had lost their truest friend, and knew not that the old song which had so often before consoled me would lead me exactly on the right way."

The old Baron, after thus suddenly hearing announced the death of the wife whom he had so secretly, but still so tenderly and fervently loved, gazed long and fixedly into the night. He leaned his head upon the casement, and finally his lips began to move; he spoke quite softly to himself, but the musician's delicate ear distinguished the words: "O how happy I might have been with thee!"

Soon, however, recovering himself and endeavoring to conceal his emotion, he addressed his confidant in solemn and subdued tones: "The body of my wife must be placed in the family vault under the castle. No one must come except the pastor, the schoolmaster, the bailiff, and thou."

"With your permission," replied the musician, "there must come yet one other, namely, a cousin of yours who arrived yesterday in the town, and who wishes to speak with you upon important family affairs."

"I have no family," said the Baron, harshly.

"That is nothing to me," returned the musician, quite as harshly; "I promised your cousin that you would see him to-morrow at ten o'clock. You will not make a liar of me, — turn Fiddlehanns into Swaggerhanns! So much the less, I think, that I suffered the cousin to pay me for my mediation with you! If you do not admit him, I as an honorable man must return him his money, and that I would be loath to do."

"We are henceforth severed for ever!" said the Baron, coldly.

"No, we are not so," quietly replied the musician; "yes, if I had used the money for myself! But it was for the poor cottager dying in the wood, and his wife and children. As I was playing 'Commit thou all thy ways,' I came unwittingly near the place where he lived, and I saw that the lightning had struck his thatched roof, that his cabin was in flames, and all were lying in the open air. Could I do anything better than to go to the inn, play for money, and let your cousin pay me well for my good word with you?"

"Hanns!" cried the Baron, angrily. "Thou wretched man, and dost thou only tell me this now?"

"That comes from the owl's life you lead," replied Fiddlehanns; "he who shuts himself up is rightly served when others are before him. Your cousin, the bailiff, the school-master, and all their kin are now down in the wood with beds and clothing, and the innkeeper has consented to receive the dying man beneath his own roof. There would be plenty of space in this old castle for more than *one* poor sick man; but no, here the owls and the bats must have all the space to themselves, all the year round."

"Out of my sight!" cried the Baron, almost beside himself with rage; "thou too hast now some design upon me! I am right: you are all good for nothing, — all, all — "

"Even she, who after an absence of more

than twenty years will return to-morrow to the castle," said the musician, who knew well how to deal with the old recluse.

The Baron was a long time silent, but finally called out in a steady voice — the firmness of which, however, was evidently forced — the following order: "To morrow at ten let the hearse stand before the drawbridge! As the clock strikes, mind you! Two days shall the coffin remain open in the chapel. And one thing more: the cousin may come too. Good night!"

Thus saying, he closed the window.

Fiddlehanns gazed long and thoughtfully toward the spot whence the Baron had spoken with him. He loved his lord above all else in the world, and the noble heart beating in that ill-shapen body was filled with a truth and purity, a boundless devotion, such as the recluse, who had been most bitterly deceived in the so-called aristocratic world, had never elsewhere encountered. The old Baron had never imparted to him the immediate causes of his misanthropy, — but Fiddlehanns had divined them. He too, poor fellow, had not had

less cause to hate his kind, for his early deform-
ity had rendered him the object of the bitterest
scorn, and even sometimes of actual abuse;
and yet he *loved* all men for the sake of the
one man, the Baron, whom he was accustomed
to call the preserver of his life, and to whom
he owed far more than the preservation of his
bodily existence.

He had been born a serf upon one of the
Hammerstone estates, and the Baron's father,
a proud man deeply imbued with all the prej-
udices of his class, and with cold-blooded se-
verity, availing himself of its immemorial but
tyrannical privileges, had determined that the
deformed boy should in future play the part of
a buffoon in the baronial castle; for it was at
that time a fancy of the lesser lords to imitate
the courts of the greater, in all their folly
and extravagance; and in emulation of kings,
princes, and dukes, counts and barons (who
plumed themselves as much upon their couple
of square miles as the former upon their larger
territories) insisted upon keeping their standing armies of two or three soldiers, their court
chapels, court households, and court fools.

The poor humpbacked boy looked forward
in despair to a fate of which he had already
had some foretaste in unworthy treatment received from the high-born youths who occasionally visited his lord's castle. Amid their
insulting words, rude jests, and ruder blows,
— all of which he was compelled to bear in
uncomplaining silence, — he felt utterly forsaken by all the world, and often envied the
baronial hounds, which, if also misused, were
at least not mocked at or derided. The proud
old Baron's son was the only living creature
who seemed to have the least sympathy with
the poor deformed boy; he often protected him
against the ill usage of his companions, always
treated him as a human being, and when he
had been unable to save him from the consequences of some rude game, would creep in
the evening to the side of the weeping boy and
endeavor to console him. Sometimes even
he would appoint a meeting in the wood,
where they could undisturbed enjoy the music of their little concerts.

When the young Baron, at his father's
death, came into possession of the estates,

his first act was to free the poor humpback. The young lord soon after went upon his travels, and the musician earned his bread by journeying from village to village, and playing at all festivals, weddings, church consecrations, and anniversaries; he thus gradually received the name of Fiddlehanns. He never forgot how his young benefactor had ever treated him as a human being, and had crowned all by bestowing upon him the most precious of gifts, freedom. He thence called him his preserver, and more than once, when he felt in especially good spirits, had he cried out: "O, if God would only grant me the favor of going through fire and water for the Baron, if I could only break my neck, or at least a leg or an arm, in his service, so that I should not be forced to leave the world his debtor!"

It gave him the deepest pain to see how his benefactor had been injured or deceived by his fellow-men, — how irremediably he had been wounded in his very life's core; it was his greatest pride that he enjoyed the confidence of the unhappy man, who had thus withdrawn himself from all association with his kind, sufficiently to be intrusted with the many acts of beneficence of which he was the secret author.

Now as he descended the hill, he again thought of his youth, of all he owed to the recluse, of the latter's profound melancholy, and of that hour which was indeed rarely absent from his mind, when the Baron would be surprised in his voluntary captivity by some malady or sudden accident, without a single friend near to aid or console him.

The moon which had just emerged from a heavy cloud, was now shining clearly upon the castle and its immediate vicinity; the old musician thought he could distinguish through the crooked branches of an aged fruit-tree a human figure. He quickly concealed himself behind the trunk of a large oak, and looked about him with a searching gaze. He soon felt convinced that the figure was that of the stranger cousin, and a suspicion which he could not stifle suddenly arose in his mind. He cautiously glided nearer the Baron's relative, and although he could see nothing un-

usual in his behavior, yet he felt very uneasy;
and when he saw him return toward the town,
he followed at a little distance, closely observ-
ing all he might do. He then carefully executed the commission intrusted to him by the
Baron.

On the following morning, as the clock
struck ten, the drawbridge was let down to
permit the passage of the hearse, which, accompanied by the pastor, the schoolmaster,
the cousin, and Fiddlehanns, already stood
without. The bailiff was not there; he had
taken a severe cold the preceding evening
from exposure to the night air in the damp
wood, and was suffering from an attack of his
old malady, rheumatism. He begged Fiddlehanns to present his excuses to the Baron;
but the latter, still greatly excited, would take
no excuse, and cried out to Fiddlehanns: "Go
back again! Have the horses harnessed; —
if he cannot walk, he must ride. He was
at the wedding, and he shall be at the home
bringing. Well, — what are you standing
there for? Are you, too, refractory? O
all is vain, — there is neither love nor truth

upon the face of this wide earth! He must come, he shall come; I will it, just because he does not wish it. Rheumatism? Miserable excuse! Any one could give the same. March!"

"By your leave!" said Fiddlehanns, gently, pressing somewhat nearer to the old lord; but the latter would not suffer him to continue, and hastily crying out, "Five feet from my person!" stepped back out of the reach of of a whispered word.

"But it is something of the greatest importance," continued the musician in imploring tones, to which the Baron was totally unaccustomed from his lips, and which only increased his ill-humor. "March!" cried he, imperiously. "You will either bring the bailiff with you, or you will never let me see you again. Our solemnities are waiting. In the meantime, I will settle matters with this cousin of mine."

The musician sadly glided away. The Baron signed to his cousin to follow him to the tower; but as he entered his chamber, and the stranger prepared to follow, the old man suddenly shut the door in his face, bolted it, then opened the sliding panel and said: "Now, sir, what do you want with me?" The cousin began a long series of friendly wishes and representations, the sum of which was, that the Baron had better abandon his strange mode of life, and pass the remainder of his days in the society of his own people. The old man laughed derisively, and replied: "Our cousin is probably a doctor; he doubtless has a diploma! Does he wish to cure me? O, I understand that much better; wait a moment!"

He left him an instant alone, then returning to the opening, handed him a full purse, adding: "We will change parts. I will play the doctor. You are suffering under a very serious malady; you are troubled with *debts*, are you not? Here is a remedy that will work an instant cure. Only no relapse, master cousin, no return! And now master cousin,—march!"

The panel was again closed. Swinging the purse in his hand, the cousin went slowly and carefully down the winding stairs; but instead

of going into the open court-yard, he hid himself in a dark passage leading to the chambers
on the ground floor.

After the lapse of a half-hour, the carriage
returned with the bailiff and the musician,
and no sooner had the old Baron heard the
rumbling of the wheels, than he descended
from the tower, and carefully and affectionately assisted the bailiff out of the vehicle.
Then, aided by Fiddlehanns, the schoolmaster,
and the two coachmen, he lifted the coffin
from the hearse and bore it into the castle
chapel, in the centre of which stood an an-
cient bier, on which the coffin was laid, and
then opened. The old man could no longer
control the feelings which, by a powerful effort,
he had hitherto suppressed ; tears gushed from
his eyes, and he sank on his knees beside the
dead.

The few words spoken by the pastor were
simple, heartfelt, and most touching ; but they
lasted far too long for Fiddlehanns. Scarcely
had the pastor concluded, when the humpbacked musician in unutterable anxiety rushed
up to the Baron, seized him by both his hands,

and asked after the cousin. The old man silently motioned him back ; but Fiddlehanns repeated the question so urgently that all the bystanders became attentive, and even infected with his alarm, more especially as they had not seen the cousin leave the castle.

The old lord meanwhile recovered his self-command. Rising from the ground, he said to the assembled retainers: " I will make my will, and you shall be the witnesses."

The musician whispered a question in the pastor's ear, and as the latter shook his head in reply, Fiddlehanns suddenly left the chapel. In vain did the Baron angrily call him to return ; he was not to be detained.

The company, led by the lord of the castle, then left the chapel, the doors of which were carefully closed, and entered a large hall. The Baron bade them wait there five minutes, and then disappeared through a small side door to bring paper, ink, and pens from the innermost recesses of his hermitage, into which no one was ever suffered to penetrate.

Scarcely had he left the hall, when those remaining behind heard a piercing cry, which

seemed to come from the ground floor. Hor-
ror-stricken, they hurried out in the direction
of the sound.

"That was certainly the voice of Fiddlehanns," said the schoolmaster; "he has met
with some accident. Come, let us aid him!
But where can he be?"

The bailiff, who was the most familiar with
all the turns in the old castle, struck at once
into the right way, and the others were just
about to follow, when the cry was repeated, but
weaker than before. The bailiff and his companions redoubled their pace, and were already
in the lower hall, when the cousin rushed past
them. They held him fast; he tried to tear
himself away and force a passage through his
captors. They stormed him with questions regarding Fiddlehanns; meantime, he succeeded
in throwing them off; he drew a pistol from
his breast, fired it, and ran away. All stood
quite astounded, when the old Baron made
his appearance, and asked, quite breathless,
"What has happened?"

When told all that was known, he cried:
"What do I care for my cousin, what for the

whole world! Seek the fiddler! My life for his!"

He forced them all out of the hall, and they soon found old Fiddlehanns in the same little room in which he had discovered the hidden cousin; — the poor humpback lay in his blood upon the floor. When he heard them coming, he raised himself slowly up, and when he beheld the Baron's tall, gaunt form, and deathly pale countenance, he gasped for breath and cried: "God be praised! He lives!" His ugly features were transfigured with joy. The Baron hastened to his side, and folding his arms tenderly around his dying form, said: "O thou, my only friend in this world, what has happened to thee?"

"Nothing," replied Fiddlehanns, gently; "the fervent wish which I have all my life kept hidden within my inmost soul has finally been gratified: I longed to die for my preserver, my benefactor."

Thus saying, he looked up into the Baron's face and smiled.

"Die!" cried the old man; "no, that thou shalt not, thou must not."

21

The musician sank back into his arms, and in broken tones replied: "Old stiff-neck! All is not in this world as you will. There is One above who also has His will, and what He does is well done. An old instrument wears out and breaks, — what more? — I have but one request!"

"Speak!" cried the Baron; "any request from thee shall be sacred to me; I will fulfil it."

"You have so many children," murmured the dying musician, — "all the people on your barony, — and they all love their good, true father so dearly! — Do as I do! Go out! I am going out of this miserable ruined cabin called life. Go you out of your captivity, out of your old tower, to your children! Long, long may you live among those whom you have aided and benefited, — you owe it to those poor people, — *her* poor people. Every heart feels oppressed when it must ever receive love which it has no opportunity of returning, when it cannot show its gratitude even by a silent glance! And when you come to die, then will true love close your eyes."

These words were his last.

"All is over!" said the pastor; the Baron himself closed the eyes of the faithful dead, sighed deeply, and then said: "Oh! there lies dead the noblest of human hearts, and so soon after that other heart which I so fervently loved. Have compassion on a poor man who now stands in this world alone and utterly desolate!"

"Not so!" returned the pastor and the bailiff; "you do not know how rich you are in love. O, remember the last prayer of our departed friend, and you will soon learn to know the full value of the treasure you possess."

"What I have promised the dead, I will perform to the living," said the old man, sinking upon the ground utterly exhausted and overcome by these sudden and repeated blows.

Meanwhile, unusual sounds were heard proceeding from the court-yard, which was soon filled by a multitude of the townspeople, who had captured the cousin and now held him a prisoner in their midst. All his efforts to escape had been in vain. When the Baron

had sent the faithful Fiddlehanns for the sick
bailiff, the musician, divining some evil, had
called together a number of the townspeople
and sent them to guard the exit of the drawbridge, impressing upon them that they were
to keep themselves concealed, and if the stranger should attempt to leave the castle, they
were to seize him, and under no circumstances
suffer him to depart, but to bring him back
again into the stronghold.

The fugitive had in fact fallen into their
hands, and the investigation instituted by the
bailiff on the spot soon brought out the whole
truth of the matter. The stranger was no
relation to the old Baron, but the leader of
a band of robbers which had long rendered the
borders of the barony insecure. He had heard
of the solitary life led by the wealthy but misanthropic recluse, and had devised a plan of
procuring access to him by feigning himself to
be a cousin. All that he saw and heard convinced him of the exceeding difficulty of exe-
cuting this project, and when the old Baron
handed him the purse through the open window, he determined to conceal himself within

the castle walls, and during the night murder and rob the recluse. Fiddlehanns had found out his hiding-place and had given the alarm, whereupon the robber had plunged his dagger into the poor musician's breast. The criminal was fettered, and delivered into the hands of justice.

The old Baron had the body of the faithful Fiddlehanns carried into the chapel and placed by the side of his wife. At the end of the time appointed, both corpses were borne into the vault, and so placed that a vacant space was left between them for the old man himself. Instead of the family escutcheon, the Baron had a silver plate inserted in the old musician's coffin, on which was inscribed: "Humanity is the loftiest Nobility!"

Notwithstanding its difficulty and his own repugnance, the gray-haired recluse faithfully kept the promise he had made to his dying friend. He left the castle and went to live with the pastor in the town where, surrounded by the unfeigned love and reverence of those whom he was never weary of benefiting, he gradually lost his misanthropy, and finally, during the last days of his life, experienced that delightful feeling which thrills a father's soul when he can look round him and behold among his grateful children the happy and ennobling effects of his own upright desires and endeavors.

Every evening, accompanied by the pastor, the old Baron went to the castle, and while the pastor awaited him in the court-yard, he remained a short time in the chapel, and played on his flute the melodies which Fiddle-hanns had been wont to accompany with his violin.

THE END.